MW00532431

A Mexican Trilogy

Faith, Hope, & Charity

Evelina Fernández

FOUNDED 1830

SAMUELFRENCH.COM
SAMUELFRENCH-LONDON.CO.UK

MUSIC USE NOTE

Licensees are solely responsible for obtaining formal written permission from copyright owners to use copyrighted music in the performance of this play and are strongly cautioned to do so. If no such permission is obtained by the licensee, then the licensee must use only original music that the licensee owns and controls. Licensees are solely responsible and liable for all music clearances and shall indemnify the copyright owners of the play(s) and their licensing agent, Samuel French, against any costs, expenses, losses and liabilities arising from the use of music by licensees. Please contact the appropriate music licensing authority in your territory for the rights to any incidental music.

IMPORTANT BILLING AND CREDIT REQUIREMENTS

If you have obtained performance rights to this title, please refer to your licensing agreement for important billing and credit requirements.

PLAYWRIGHT'S NOTE

There are so many stories that need to be told. Most of my plays are about people I know or things I've experienced first hand. I felt compelled to write *A Mexican Trilogy* because of the anti-immigrant sentiment in the U.S. that has intensified in this new millennium. The stories, which span over 100 years, are loosely based on my family, past and present. It is my hope that this trilogy will play a small part in creating understanding of those who come to this country to make a better life, to work, to contribute, to dream of a brighter future for future generations and who permeate the American fabric and our way of life.

PRODUCTION

A Mexican Trilogy: Faith, Hope, and Charity is written so that each part can be performed individually or collectively. It is possible to perform the entire trilogy with a company of 11 actors: 3 female (teens – 20s), 2 male (teens – 20s), 3 female (30 – 50s), 3 male (30-50s).

Individually, cast sizes are:

FAITH: 9 actors [3 female (teens), 2 male (teens), 2 female (30 - 40s), 2 male (40s)].

HOPE: 8 actors [2 female (teens), 2 male (teens), 2 female (30 – 40s), 2 male (30 – 40s)].

CHARITY: 9 actors [1 female (teen -20s), 2 male (20s), 3 female (40 – 50s), 3 male (40 – 50s)].

The characters range from recent immigrants to first, second and third generation Americans spanning over a hundred years. The plays are written primarily in English, with most of the characters speaking bilingually (Spanish and English). Italicized words (other than translations) mean to use Spanish pronunciation. For example: "Los Angeles" (use Spanish pronunciation), Los Angeles (use English pronunciation). Spanish and English pronunciations change from character to character, depending on the level of assimilation. If an actor is not bilingual, it is preferable for the character to use the English translation dialogue rather than to mispronounce the Spanish and compromise the authenticity of the characters.

PRONUNCIATION AND ACCENTS

It is important that the Spanish pronunciation in the trilogy is specifically Mexican. Immigrant characters such as Silvestre, Esperanza and Lupe in "Faith" should have accents when speaking English. However, first generation characters such as Faith, Charity, Elena, Freddie and Charlie should only have slight accents or no accents at all when speaking English. In "Hope," Elena, Carlos (Charlie) and Enrique are first generation Mexican-Americans and should have slight or no accents. Mari, on the other hand, a Mexican immigrant, should have an accent when speaking English. In "Charity," only Esperanza, Silvestre and the recently arrived, Francisco, should have accents. All the other characters are second and third generation Mexican-Americans and should have no accents when speaking English.

MUSIC AND FOOTAGE

The music and footage in the plays are integral to each part of trilogy, as it sets the three parts in a specific time in U.S. history and within an American context. The songs that are sung by specific characters also helps identify their degree of assimilation.

A MEXICAN TRILOGY

Faith

Part I

(1915, 1940 – 1944)

FAITH: PART I OF A MEXICAN TRILOGY was first produced by the Latino Theater Company in Los Angeles, CA on October 13, 2012 at the Los Angeles Theatre Center. The performance was directed by Jose Luis Valenzuela, with sets, lights, and projections by Cameron Mock, costumes by Carlos Brown, choreography by Urbanie Lucero, and music by Rosino Serrano. The Production Stage Manager was Henry "Heno" Fernandez. The cast was as follows:

YOUNG ESPERANZA	Olivia Delgado
YOUNG SILVESTRE (PRIEST)	Matias Ponce
ESPERANZA	Lucy Rodriguez
SILVESTRE	Sal Lopez
FAITH	Esperanza America
CHARITY	Alexis de la Rocha
ELENA	Olivia Delgado
CHARLIE	Xavi Moreno
FREDDIE	Matias Ponce
LUPE	Evelina Fernandez

CHARACTERS

GRANDMOTHER – 60, she imparts the ancient words of wisdom handed down from her ancestors. (Can be double cast by the actor who plays Lupe)

YOUNG ESPERANZA – 15, she is strong and determined to get the man she loves. (Can be double cast by the actor who plays Elena)

YOUNG SILVESTRE (PRIEST) – 20, runs away with Young Esperanza. (Can be double cast by the actor who plays Freddie.)

ESPERANZA – 30s, grown with three daughters. She tries to raise her daughters with an iron hand while her husband works in the mine.

SILVESTRE – 40, Esperanza's husband, is a copper miner and becoming disillusioned with the working conditions. He begins to organize the miners.

FAITH – 16, their oldest daughter, is as strong willed and determined as Esperanza. She wants to be a singer more than anything else in the world.

CHARITY – 15, their middle daughter, is patriotic and loves President Franklin Delano Roosevelt and wants to be American, not Mexican.

ELENA – 13, their youngest daughter is stuck between childhood and womanhood. She pees in bed, farts in her sleep and can't keep a secret.

LUPE – 50, Esperanza's friend and confidant, has sensuous thoughts about men and flirts with Ricardo Flores. She is left to watch the girls when Esperanza has to return to Mexico.

RICARDO FLORES – 40, a local radio personality who promises to make Faith's dreams come true.

FREDDIE – 18, falls in love with Charity and leaves to fight in WWII.

CHARLIE – 15, has a mad crush on Faith, but she thinks he's a kid.

SETTING & TIME

1915 – A small town in Mexico

1940-1944 – A small mining town in northern Arizona

Prologue, Part One

México, 1915

(Music up: Náhuatl Indian drum, conch shell, flutes...)

(Lights up on a young woman, **YOUNG ESPERANZA**, *15, in a white dress, long braids and huaraches. She is in the center of a coming of age ceremony surrounded by women. They recite the ancient words of wisdom:)*

WOMEN. You have arrived, my little girl, precious necklace, precious feather. You came to life, you were born; our Creator and our mother sent you to earth. This is a place of thirst, a place of hunger. This is how things are. Listen my daughter and learn how to live upon the earth. How should you live? Remember that one does not live easily upon this earth. But do not forget, that above all you have come from someone, that you are descended from someone, that you were born by the grace of someone; that you are both the spine and the offspring of our ancestors, of those who came before us, and of those who have gone on to live in the great beyond.

(They touch her head in a blessing. **YOUNG ESPERANZA***'s* **GRANDMOTHER**, *the eldest of the women, speaks.)*

GRANDMOTHER. Esperanza.

YOUNG ESPERANZA. *¿Sí, Nana? (Yes, Nana?)*

GRANDMOTHER. The women in this family cannot lie. A promise was made many years ago. Do not lie or make up stories or it will go very badly for you.

YOUNG ESPERANZA. *Sí, Nana. (Yes, Nana.)*

(Sound cue: Náhuatl Indian drums and flutes)

(The group of women exit dancing a traditional Náhuatl Indian dance.)

(Sound fades out.)

Prologue, Part Two

(Sound cue: a guitar plays "La Valentina," an old Mexican song from the turn of the 20th Century)

(YOUNG ESPERANZA is confessing to a priest. She crosses herself.)

YOUNG ESPERANZA. Bless me father for I have sinned. It has been one day since my last confession.

PRIEST. One day, my child?

YOUNG ESPERANZA. Yes, father.

PRIEST. How much can you sin in one day?

YOUNG ESPERANZA. *(sigh)* Plenty. But, how can one control one's thoughts, one's imagination?

PRIEST. I understand.

YOUNG ESPERANZA. *(whispers)* I can't stop thinking about the man I love. His eyes, his face, his hands, his body...

(The priest breathes hard.)

PRIEST. You can't...

YOUNG ESPERANZA. Why not? He's a man and I'm a woman...

PRIEST. It's a sin.

YOUNG ESPERANZA. No! To love is not a sin! The sin is this wretched war that is destroying us all! The sin is the hunger that is killing us. To love is not a sin. It's a sin not to love. It's a sin not to be able to love the person who loves you.

(YOUNG ESPERANZA and the PRIEST embrace, they kiss and run off together.)

ACT ONE

Scene One
A small mining town in Arizona, 1940

(Music up: an Andrews Sisters song from 1940, "Sing, Sing, Sing.")

(Lights up on a radio in the Morales house. Three beautiful girls, **FAITH***, 16,* **CHARITY***, 15, and* **ELENA** *13, with braids and bows in their hair, sing along with the radio while they hem white sheets. Their mother,* **ESPERANZA***, now in her 40s, sits with them while* **FAITH** *sits at the table,* **CHARITY** *sits next to the radio and* **ELENA** *sits on the floor in the middle of the stage. They are embroidering.* **ESPERANZA***'s comadre,* **LUPE***, 50s, stands next to the radio.)*

*(***FAITH***,* **CHARITY***, and* **ELENA** *sing the first twelve lines from "Sing, Sing, Sing.")*

(Sound cue: radio)

RICARDO FLORES VOICE ON RADIO. *Buenas tardes, damas y caballeros.* Good afternoon ladies and gentlemen. Today is December 29, 1940 *y les habla su servidor, Ricardo Flores. (this is your humble servant, Ricardo Flores.)* I am Ricardo Flores, but for those of you who prefer the American language, you can call me...

FAITH, CHARITY, ELENA. ...Ricky Flowers.

RICARDO FLORES. And now let's listen to the sisters we all love, the Andrews Sisters.

---

*Please see Music Use note on page 3

17

(Sound cue: the Andrews Sisters music plays softly.*)*

ESPERANZA. When I was a girl I would dream that I was swept up by a wave that would take me away to a far away land where everything and everyone was different. I wanted to get away from my town, from *México*, from the violence, the poverty, the shame of not having enough to eat. When Silvestre and I came north it was like my dream had come true.

LUPE. Ay, Esperanza. That's what I miss most about being young, dreaming…

*(***LUPE*** sits next to ***ESPERANZA*** and lights a hand made cigarette.)*

ELENA. *Mamá*, tell Doña Lupe about my *tío* fighting with Emiliano Zapata.

LUPE. Your brother fought in the revolution?

ESPERANZA. Yes, he fought with Emiliano Zapata, against my parents wishes. We were not poor. On the contrary, we always had food and clothes and animals, chickens, pigs… But, the Revolution changed all that. The Revolution took our house, took our land, took our life. The worst thing is that we were in favor of the Revolution. But, to those who were fighting for justice, we were what they were fighting against. No, questions were asked. If it looked like you had something, it was taken away. Revolutions are always messy that way and many times the road to justice is…unjust. I know this now, but not then.

(silence)

My brother was kind, like all the men in our family. He always felt sorry for the less fortunate. I saw him as he snuck away that night to get a closer look at the camp and at Emiliano. I watched him disappear into the darkness. But, I never imagined that he would never come back. My father never forgave him. My mother begged him to please let him come home, but my

---

* Please see Music Use note on page 3

father refused. My father died and they never saw each other again. Never embraced each other again.

LUPE. *Ay, qué lástima.* What a shame…

ELENA. Doña Lupe, did you know that *mamá's* family were Indians?

LUPE. *¿De veras? (Really?)*

(**FAITH** *and* **CHARITY** *roll their eyes at* **ELENA.**)

ESPERANZA. Yes, they were *Náhuatl.* They knew the language and they blessed me with their words of wisdom.

FAITH. Did they kill cowboys with bows and arrows, too?

ESPERANZA. No, they did not, *¡malcriada! (ill-bred!)*

CHARITY. We know, they were wise and dignified.

FAITH. You told us all about them.

ESPERANZA. It's the truth. But, of course none of you appreciate your heritage. You make fun of it, disparage it. This country has caused a degeneration of this family.

FAITH. What can I say, Mom. You should have stayed in Mexico.

ESPERANZA. Don't you say that to me, *¡hija de la tiznada! (daughter of darkness!)* You know why we left! We left because we were starving, because we lost everything! We left because my grandmother died of horror and because my little sister died of starvation. That's why we left! We had no choice.

LUPE. *Déjala, comadre, (Leave her alone, my friend,)* you know how young people are. Don't you ever want to go back? How long has it been since you've seen your mother?

ESPERANZA. Over twenty years.

LUPE. *¡Válgame Dios! (Good heavens!)*

ESPERANZA. I sometimes wonder what it would be like to go back. I am sure it has changed. And I have changed. I suppose I prefer the myth of the past, to the truth of the present.

LUPE. *Sí, entiendo. (Yes, I understand.)* There's no money to go back. We barely have enough to eat.

ESPERANZA. If it were not for President Roosevelt we would have starved to death. I still have a sack of flour they gave us, remember? I saved it, just in case, because you never know... We wouldn't have anything if it were not for him.

FAITH. We still have holes in our shoes.

ESPERANZA. You are lucky you have shoes.

CHARITY. And thank God that we live in the best country in the world. President Roosevelt says we all have to sacrifice together..

FAITH. I don't like wearing old shoes with holes in them. It's embarrassing.

ESPERANZA. *Ay, sí tú. (Oh, I'm sure.)*

CHARITY. I don't care. Everyone has old shoes.

FAITH. Not this old. My toes are all scrunched up.

ESPERANZA. *Cállate. (Be quiet.)* Don't complain. At least you have a roof over your head and food on the table. *Malagradecida. (Ungrateful.)*

LUPE. *Déjala... (Leave her alone...)* Ignacio has been talking about going back to *México* because he doesn't want to keep working in the mines. He has trouble breathing and he has a cough that keeps us up at night. Why do you think I have these *ojeras*, these bags under my eyes.

ELENA. Let me see?

ESPERANZA. Elena.

ELENA. Oh, yes, they are big... *Mamá* says you look old because you smoke and you drink *tequila.*

ESPERANZA. Elena!

LUPE. *Déjala...* It's true. *Ay, comadre,* I don't want to go back to *México.* But Ignacio's afraid they'll deport him like they deported his father. I don't know... He says Silvestre is getting too involved in the problems in the mine. He thinks he'll get in trouble. Ignacio doesn't want anything to do with the union. He's not as brave as Silvestre. He's too old...

ELENA. Yes, he looks like he's your father.

ESPERANZA. Elena!

LUPE. *Déjala… (Leave her alone.)*

ESPERANZA. My husband is too good. Always worried about his fellow man. I don't like him getting involved but if he sees an injustice…

LUPE. He should be careful. If he loses his job, what will you do?

ESPERANZA. I know.

ELENA. *Mamá, dile a la comadre la historia (Mom, tell her the story)* about what happened to my *abuelita. Esa sí que está buena. (Now, that's a good one.)*

ESPERANZA. *¡Ya les dije que no anden con esa lengua de chu chu! (I've already told you not to speak in the devil's tongue!)* Either you speak Spanish or you speak English. But, not both at the same time.

ELENA. *Sí, mamá.*

(Silence. They go back to the embroidering.)

LUPE. *Comadre, (Dear friend,)* it's not their fault. They hit them at school if they speak Spanish and you get mad if they speak English with Spanish. *Pobrecitas, (Poor things,)* they're gonna go mute.

ELENA. Like your daughter?

(ESPERANZA smacks ELENA.)

ESPERANZA. Elena! *Vas a ver… (You'll see…)*

LUPE. *Déjala… (Leave her alone…)* It's true. My daughter can't speak. That's why that boy… Who knows why God has punished me.

ESPERANZA. God doesn't punish, *comadre.* God sends us challenges.

LUPE. He punished me for being stupid and for running around… *(She looks at the girls and stops herself.)* Well, you know…

ESPERANZA. We all make mistakes when we're young *comadre.* We all make mistakes…

LUPE. I used to be young and stupid and now... I'm old and stupid.

ESPERANZA. It's not true.

LUPE. It is. You're not gonna believe it *comadre*, but sometimes I see a man in the street and I start imagining things. Maybe because Ignacio is so old and well..

ESPERANZA. *Ay, comadre... (Oh, dear friend.)*

(**ELENA** *laughs loud.* **ESPERANZA** *gives her a look. She stops.*)

LUPE. *Bueno, comadre, ya me voy. (Well, friend, I'm leaving.)* Ignacio will be home for dinner soon. *(She picks up a small bottle from the table.)* Thank you for the poison. I have to get rid of those ugly rats. I don't know what I would do without you, *comadrita. (little friend.)*

ESPERANZA. *No hay de qué... (There's no need...)*

(**ESPERANZA** *exits upstage left door and* **LUPE** *exits downstage left door.*)

(*Audio: Franklin Delano Roosevelt's Second Inaugural Address, December 29, 1940, FDR Fireside Chat*)

FDR. It was a time when the wheels of American industry were grinding to a full stop, when the whole banking system of our country had ceased to function.

I had before my eyes the picture of all those Americans with whom I was talking. I saw the workmen in the mills, the mines, the factories; the girl behind the counter; the small shopkeeper; the farmer doing his spring plowing; the widows and the old men wondering about their life's savings.

I tried to convey to the great mass of American people what the banking crisis meant to them in their daily lives.

Tonight, I want to do the same thing, with the same people, in this new crisis which faces America.

(*Radio fades out.*)

Scene Two

(The girls are listening to the radio.)

RICARDO FLORES' VOICE ON RADIO. Good morning ladies and gentlemen. *Buenos días, damas y caballeros. Les habla su servidor, Ricardo Flores, (I am your humble servant, Ricardo Flores,)* or for those of you who prefer the America language you can call me…

FAITH, CHARITY, ELENA. Ricky Flowers…

(Sound cue: radio fades down)

*(**FAITH** is sitting at the vanity stage left putting on red lipstick while **CHARITY** and **ELENA** fold sheets.)*

CHARITY. Aren't you gonna help?

FAITH. In a minute.

ELENA. I'm gonna tell Mom you put on lipstick.

FAITH. Go ahead you tattle-tale. I'm gonna tell all your friends at school that you pee in bed.

ELENA. No, don't. I won't tell her.

CHARITY. Faith, ask Mom if we can go to the d-a-n-c-e.

*(**ELENA** tries to figure out what she spelled.)*

ELENA. D-a-… what?

FAITH. Nothing you dummy. She said ask Mom if we can go to church.

ELENA. No, she didn't. You don't spell church with a "D."

FAITH. How would you know, you big dummy.

CHARITY. You can't spell.

FAITH. I'm not gonna ask her. She's going to g-e-t m-a-d.

*(**ELENA** tries to figure out what she just spelled. **FAITH** puts lipstick on **CHARITY**.)*

She's always m-a-d. She won't let us go to the f-o-o-t-b-a-l-l-g-a-m-e. She won't let us go to the da…

ELENA. Dance. That's what starts with a "D." D-a-n-c-e spells dance.

FAITH. So, you know how to spell "dance." Whoop dee do. What do you want, a prize? *(to* **CHARITY***)* I can't go to the dance in these shoes. *(She looks at her raggedy shoes.)*

CHARITY. Mom's afraid we'll get in trouble like her *comadre* Lupe's daughter, Dora. She ran away with that boy...

FAITH. Now we have to pay the consequences.

CHARITY. The whole town is talking about it. They say she's e-x-p-e-c-t-i-n-g

ELENA. I know what you're spelling,"expecting." I already know she's expecting because I heard some ladies talking about it at the store.

FAITH. Big ears. You're always eavesdropping on people's conversations and poking your nose in other people's business.

*(***ELENA** *sticks her tongue out at* **FAITH***.)*

Eww, someone smells like pee.

*(***ELENA** *smells herself.)*

ELENA. No, I don't, I took a bath.

CHARITY. Come on, Faith, ask Mom. Freddie and Charlie are gonna be there...

FAITH. Charlie? Ugh! Now, I really don't wanna go.

CHARITY. Please! There's going to be a talent contest.

*(***FAITH***'s eyes widen.)*

FAITH. There is?

CHARITY. We can sign up and we can sing.

*(***FAITH** *thinks for a sec.)*

FAITH. Okay, I'll ask her.

*(***FAITH** *looks at herself in the mirror. She begins to sing. Lights change, music comes up and the radio comes on.)*

(Sound cue: radio up. Lights up on radio personality:)

RICARDO FLORES. And now let's listen to the sisters we all love, *las Hermanas Morales. Ahí les va...* (the Morales Sisters. Here it goes...)

(Lights change and the girls are in the amateur hour in **FAITH***'s imagination, singing "I'll Never Smile Again," just like the Andrews Sisters.)*

*(***FAITH, CHARITY,*** *and* **ELENA** *sing the first seven lines of "I'll Never Smile Again."*)*

*(***ESPERANZA*** *enters. She turns off the radio. The girls scatter trying to make it look like they are busy cleaning. She sees the lipstick on* **FAITH***.)*

ESPERANZA. *¿Y eso?* What's that?

CHARITY. Nothing.

ESPERANZA. Lipstick? Ah, no. You're not going to paint your faces like streetwalkers. Who has it?

(They don't answer.)

Dime. (Tell me.) (She looks at **ELENA***.)* Tell me, Elena.

ELENA. *(She shakes her head "no.")* I can't.

ESPERANZA. Why not?

ELENA. Because Faith will tell my friends that I pee the bed.

*(***ESPERANZA*** *looks at* **FAITH***.* **FAITH** *gives up the lipstick.)*

FAITH. Here! Take it! *(She looks at* **ELENA***.)* Tattle-tale.

ELENA. I didn't tell.

CHARITY. You might as well have.

ELENA. *Mamá,* tell Faith not to tell anybody that I pee the bed.

ESPERANZA. Are you, *Fe? (Faith?)*

*(***FAITH** *doesn't answer.)*

I'm talking to you…

FAITH. Yes, I'm going to tell everyone that she pees in bed and that she's stupid and she can't spell!

*(***ELENA** *starts to cry.)*

ESPERANZA. *¡Cállate, Fe! (Be quiet, Faith!)*

FAITH. I won't be quiet!

---

*Please see Music Use note on page 3

(ESPERANZA goes to hit FAITH.)

ELENA. *¡No, mamacita! (No, little mother!)*

(ESPERANZA stops.)

ESPERANZA. *¡Híncate! (Kneel down.)*

FAITH. No, I'm not going to kneel down!

ELENA/CHARITY. *¡No, mamacita!*

(She grabs FAITH by the hair and pulls her to her knees. CHARITY and ELENA cry.)

ESPERANZA. You will not answer me that way!

FAITH. I just did.

(ESPERANZA's husband, SILVESTRE, 40s, enters stage left. He sees FAITH kneeling on the floor. The younger girls run into his arms.)

SILVESTRE. *¿Pero qué haces, mujer? ¡Por Dios! (What are you doing, woman? For God's sake!)*

(He picks up FAITH and holds her. She sobs in his arms.)

ESPERANZA. Look at them, wearing lipstick!

FAITH. *Papá,* she doesn't let us do anything. I can't go to the football games. I can't go to the dances. I'm embarrassed to go to school wearing these old shoes full of holes…

(SILVESTRE gives ESPERANZA a look.)

ESPERANZA. Don't exaggerate, Fe.

SILVESTRE. *¿A ver? (Let me see?)*

(FAITH takes off her shoes and pulls a piece of cardboard from inside one of them. CHARITY and ELENA quickly do the same.)

¡Ya ni la friegas, Esperanza! (This is too much, Esperanza!) Why haven't you bought them shoes?

ESPERANZA. We don't have any money. We barely have enough to eat.

(He looks at the girls.)

SILVESTRE. Get ready. Let's go buy you shoes.

(The girls put their shoes on quickly.)

ESPERANZA. Silvestre, we don't have the money.

(He doesn't speak, but leaves with the girls upstage left.)

*(**ESPERANZA** is left alone. Sound cue: the sound of ocean waves… She remembers.)*

When I was little, my father took us to the ocean once. I remember standing there, holding his hand as the water washed over our bare feet, looking out at that enormous body of water and I asked *papá* what was on the other side. *"El mundo,"* he said. "The world." In that moment, that instant, I became aware of my insignificance, of how small my life was. I used to dream that a wave would sweep me up and take me far away to a place where everyone and everything was different.

Scene Three

(The girls run up to the swing. They laugh and talk as they look at their new shoes, socks, dresses.)

FAITH. Dad said we could go to the dance.

CHARITY. But, Mom won't let us.

FAITH. She'll have to. He already said "yes." He's the boss.

ELENA. No, he isn't.

CHARITY. He's the man!

ELENA. But, he's not the boss.

FAITH. He is today and that's all that counts and he said we could go to the dance.

ELENA. *Mamá* is not going to let us go alone.

CHARITY. Maybe Dad will take us...

FAITH. Fat chance.

CHARITY. Mom will take us and then...

FAITH. It doesn't matter. We'll sign up for the talent contest and when they call us up, don't look at Mom just go on stage before she can stop us. Okay?

(FAITH looks at ELENA.)

FAITH. Okay?

(ELENA doesn't answer...)

If you don't...

ELENA. Okay!

FAITH. What should we sing?

CHARITY. I don't know...

ELENA. How about...

FAITH. "I'll Never Smile Again."

CHARITY. Yeah, we sing that one real good.

(FAITH starts going through their new stuff.)

FAITH. Okay, you wear this and I'll wear that. We'll pin our hair up in front in a pompadour...

CHARITY. I can't wait. I feel like the luckiest girl in the world!

(**RICARDO FLORES** *comes on the radio.*)

RICARDO FLORES. *Les habla su servidor, Ricardo Flores.* I am Ricardo Flores, but for those of you who prefer the American language, you can call me Ricky Flowers. I want to remind you all about the dance this Friday night in the high school auditorium where there will be a singing contest and where we will be dancing to our favorite American and Mexican music. And now a dedication from Bobby Sanchez from Jerome to María Martínez from Clarkdale. And now one of our all time favorites, *"Amapola." Ahí les va... (Here it goes...)"*

Scene Four

("Amapola"* plays on the radio as **ESPERANZA** *is in bed under the sheets.* **SILVESTRE** *enters and sits on the bed. She moves close to him.)*

ESPERANZA. How much did you spend?

SILVESTRE. I bought them shoes. They need them. I don't want to see them with holes in their shoes... What do I work for?

ESPERANZA. So that we can eat. *(Silence. Whispers:) Perdóname... (Forgive me...) (He doesn't answer. Louder:)* Forgive me... *(no answer)* Forgive me, I said!

SILVESTRE. *(whispers)* Quiet, Esperanza. Please, be quiet. Don't ask me for forgiveness. Ask our daughters for forgiveness. You mistreat them. Our disgrace is not their fault.

ESPERANZA. Our disgrace? Because we ran away together?

SILVESTRE. I don't want the girls to know...

ESPERANZA. ...about the sin we committed? Forgive me, Silvestre. It's all my fault...

SILVESTRE. No. *(pause)* I didn't mean... I am happy that I fell in love with you. But, when you treat the girls like that. They're little girls...

ESPERANZA. They are women now, Silvestre, and I have to take care of them. Look at what happened to Lupe's daughter, Dora.

SILVESTRE. Stop. You did the same. Just because nobody knows it, doesn't mean it didn't happen.

(He gets up to leave.)

ESPERANZA. ¿Adónde vas? *(Where are you going?)*

SILVESTRE. I have a meeting.

ESPERANZA. Again? Do you have to?

SILVESTRE. What do you want me to do, Esperanza? Do you want me to stay quiet when the men are dying

---

* Please see Music Use Note on page 3

because of the dust they have breathed in the mine for years? Look at our *compadre (dear friend)* and José Sánchez? They fired him because he was old and sick. He coughs up pieces of his lungs and it isn't right. He worked in the mine for twenty years and he has no help, no benefits.

ESPERANZA. What if you lose your job?

SILVESTRE. I'll find another.

ESPERANZA. Ay, Silvestre, why do you have to be so good?

SILVESTRE. Good? I'm not good. I'm a sinner from way back.

(He kisses her.)

Scene Five

(*Music: Glen Miller's "Chatanooga Choo Choo"**)

(**FAITH, CHARITY, ELENA, ESPERANZA** and **LUPE** are at the dance in the school auditorium. **ESPERANZA** and **LUPE** sit on a bench, keeping an eye on the girls who stand nearby. **RICARDO FLORES** enters and catches Lupe's eye. **CHARITY** goes to **ESPERANZA**.)

CHARITY. *Mamá,* can we dance?

ESPERANZA. *Sí… juntas.* (*Yes… with each other.*)

CHARITY. With each other?

FAITH. (*to* **CHARITY**) I'd rather die.

CHARITY. But…

FAITH. Be quiet.

CHARITY. Come on, it's better than nothing.

(*She pulls* **FAITH** *out on to the dance floor stage right.*)

FAITH. If someone asks me to dance, I'm dancing.

CHARITY. But…

ELENA. *¡Mamá! Dice Faith que si…* (*Mom! Faith says that if…*)

(**FAITH** *pinches her.*)

Ouch!

CHARITY. Shhh…

(**FREDDIE,** *17,* and **CHARLIE,** *15, enter.*)

(*to* **FAITH**) Here come Freddie and Charlie.

(*to* **ELENA**) I'll give you a penny if you ask Mom for a *limonada.* (*lemonade.*)

ELENA. She won't buy it for me.

FAITH. No, but maybe *comadre* Lupe will.

(**ELENA** *thinks on it and takes the penny. She goes to* **ESPERANZA** *and* **LUPE** *who are talking on a bench nearby.*)

---

* Please see Music Use note on page 3

ELENA. *Mamá, ¿me compras una limonada? (Mamá, will you buy me a lemonade?)*

ESPERANZA. No.

LUPE. *No seas mala, comadre. (Don't be mean, dear friend.)* Buy her a lemonade.

ESPERANZA. I can't afford it. I have to watch the girls.

(**LUPE** *gives her a look.*)

LUPE. *Ay, comadre, (Oh, dear friend,)* did you already forget what it was to be young? They are dancing with each other, *pobrecitas. (poor things.)* I'll buy all of us a lemonade. Come on, I think Ricardo Flores is over there. I want to say "hello." *Ándale. (Come on.)*

(**ESPERANZA** *looks at the girls then at the comadre.*)

(*Music plays: "Fools Rush In"**)

ESPERANZA. *Ándale, pues. (Alright then.)*

(**ESPERANZA, LUPE** *and* **ELENA** *exit.* **FREDDIE** *and* **CHARLIE** *approach* **FAITH** *and* **CHARITY**.)

FREDDIE. *(to* **CHARITY***)* Hi gorgeous.

CHARLIE. *(to* **FAITH***)* Hi beautiful.

(**CHARITY** *giggles,* **FAITH** *rolls her eyes.*)

FAITH/CHARITY. Hi…

FREDDIE. You wanna dance before your mother comes back?

CHARITY. Uh huh.

CHARLIE. Want to?

(**FAITH** *rolls her eyes again.*)

FAITH. Sure…

FREDDIE. You sure look pretty tonight.

CHARITY. I do?

FREDDIE. You sure do.

---

*Please see Music Use note on page 3

(Lights crossfade to **DOÑA LUPE** *as she sees* **RICARDO FLORES**.*)*

LUPE. *Buenas noches, Señor Flores.*

RICARDO FLORES. Buenas noches, *señoras.* *(to* **ELENA***)* *Señorita.* You all look lovely tonight.

*(***LUPE** *giggles.* **ESPERANZA** *is not impressed.)*

LUPE. *Gracias.* *(Thank you.)*

RICARDO FLORES. *(to* **ELENA***)* Did you sign up for the talent contest tonight?

*(***LUPE** *thinks he's talking to her.)*

LUPE. Oh, no. I haven't sang in years. Not since I was a young girl.

RICARDO FLORES. Well, that wasn't too long ago.

*(***LUPE** *giggles.)*

LUPE. Oh, Mr. Flores.

(He looks at his watch.)

RICARDO FLORES. Excuse me, *señoras.* I hope you have a lovely night.

LUPE. Thank you.

(He exits. **LUPE** *looks at* **ESPERANZA**.*)*

Isn't he handsome?

ESPERANZA. He's not my type.

(Lights crossfade to the girls are dancing with **FREDDIE** *and* **CHARLIE**.*)*

FREDDIE. Hey, what do you say I come over your house?

CHARITY. No!

FREDDIE. No, why?

CHARITY. My Mom's really strict.

FREDDIE. I can try to talk to her.

CHARITY. No! No, please don't do that.

FREDDIE. Okay.

*(***CHARLIE** *is dancing with* **FAITH**.*)*

CHARLIE. Can I kiss you?

FAITH. No. *(She pulls away a little from him. Her mind is somewhere else.)* I wonder when the talent contest is.

CHARLIE. Why not?

FAITH. Why not what?

CHARLIE. Why can't I kiss you?

FAITH. Because my mother's here and besides I don't like you that way?

(He's crushed.)

CHARLIE. Why not?

FAITH. I don't know, I just don't.

CHARLIE. But…

FAITH. You're a kid. I like the older type.

CHARLIE. I'm almost sixteen.

FAITH. A kid. You should date my little sister, Elena.

*(**CHARLIE** looks at her.)*

CHARLIE. She's a baby.

FAITH. So are you.

MUSIC OUT

*(**RICARDO FLORES** goes to the microphone.)*

RICARDO FLORES. *¡Buenas noches, damas y caballeros!* Good evening, ladies and gentlemen. I am your humble servant, Ricky Flowers; *su servidor, Ricardo Flores.* And now, the time we have all been waiting for, the talent contest. I have the names of the people who have signed up and the first singer is… *¡Las Hermanas Morales!*

(The girls look at each other. They go to the stage. They sing "I'll Never Smile Again" just like the Andrews Sisters.*)

---

*Please see Music Use note on page 3

(**FAITH, CHARITY,** *and* **ELENA** *sing the first seven lines of "I'll Never Smile Again."**)

(**ESPERANZA** *enters and sees the girls onstage.*)

ESPERANZA. *¡Estas cabronas!* (*These damned girls!*)

(*She begins to head toward the stage, but comadre* **LUPE** *stops her.*)

LUPE. No, *comadre.* You'll embarrass them too much. Don't do it.

(**ESPERANZA** *stops.*)

(**FAITH, CHARITY,** *and* **ELENA** *sing the next eight lines of "I'll Never Smile Again."**)

(*The song ends.*)

(*Sound cue: applause*)

(**ESPERANZA** *goes to the girls and leads them out of the auditorium.*)

RICARDO FLORES. *(onstage mic)* Let's hear it again for *Las Hermanas Morales*! Weren't they terrific? Now, let's hear it for our wonderful band, Manny Fernández and his trio. I want to remind everyone about the Amateur Hour we have once a month down at the radio station where only the most talented are invited to sing live. Now, our next contestant is Millie Martínez and her sassy saxophone.

(*Sound cue: applause.*)

---

* Please see Music Use note on page 3

Scene Six

(**SILVESTRE** *is laughing at the story that* **ESPERANZA** *is telling him.*)

ESPERANZA. They got on the stage and sang a song.

SILVESTRE. *¿Mexicana o Americana? (Mexican or American?)*

ESPERANZA. *Americana. Una de que, (American. One that says,)* "I smile or never smile…"

(*He laughs some more.*)

SILVESTRE. And they won?

ESPERANZA. *Sí!*

SILVESTRE. *No me digas. (You don't say.)* Well, they took after you because I…

ESPERANZA. …you were a saint. *Ni tan santo. (Not such a saint.)*

(*They kiss. He tries to touch her breasts. She slaps his hand.*)

SILVESTRE. Who can understand you? First you want to and then…

ESPERANZA. Shhh… the girls.

SILVESTRE. They are sound asleep. Did they have a good time?

ESPERANZA. Yes, a very good time.

SILVESTRE. Good. That's the way it should be, isn't it?

ESPERANZA. No. They should be good students and..

SILVESTRE. …and enjoy their youth. Look at us. The revolution took our childhood away. We were two children who ran away together…

ESPERANZA. We had to grow up…

SILVESTRE. We grew up too fast.

ESPERANZA. But, my mother was strict. She raised me to be a nice young lady, with good manners…

SILVESTRE. And look what happened!

ESPERANZA. *Hijo de tu… (Son of a…)*

SILVESTRE. Watch your mouth, woman…

ESPERANZA. Well, don't make me mad…

(He embraces her. He babies her.)

SILVESTRE. *A ver la carita…* (*Let me see your little face…*)

(ESPERANZA shakes her head "no.")

Ándale… (Come on…)

(She looks at him.)

You're as pretty as the day I fell in love with you.

(They kiss.)

(SILVESTRE sings six lines of "Llegando a ti" by José Alfredo Jiménez.)*

(ESPERANZA joins in.)

(SILVESTRE and ESPERANZA sing four lines together.)*

---

*Please see Music Use note on page 3

Scene Seven

(**CHARLIE** *and* **FREDDIE** *are outside the window.*)

CHARLIE. Faith! Faith!

FREDDIE. Charity!

(**CHARITY** *comes to the window.*)

CHARITY. Faith, come on, it's Freddie and Charlie.

FAITH. What? I told him, I don't like him.

(**FAITH** *comes to the balcony.*)

Charlie, what are you doing? I already told you.

CHARLIE. Come on, Faith, give me a chance.

FAITH. No, get out of here. You're gonna get us in trouble…

(**FREDDIE** *and* **CHARLIE** *begin to serenade singing five lines from "Llegando a ti."*)

(**ESPERANZA** *comes out of the house with a broom and swats the boys away.*)

ESPERANZA. ¡Ándenle! ¡Fuera de aquí! ¡Váyanse! (*Go on! Get out of here! Go on!*)

FAITH/CHARITY. ¡Mamá!

(*The boys run away.*)

---

*Please see Music Use note on page 3

Scene Eight

(*Lights up* **CHARITY** *listening to the radio and* **RICARDO FLORES** *in the studio.*)

RICARDO FLORES. *Buenos días, damas y caballeros. (Good morning, ladies and gentlemen.)* Today is May 27, 1941. And now a word from our president.

FDR. The pressing problems that confront us are military and naval problems. We cannot afford to approach them from the point of view of wishful thinkers or sentimentalists. What we face is cold, hard fact.

There first and fundamental fact is that what started as a European war has developed, as the Nazis always intended it should develop, into a world war for world domination.

(*She turns the radio off.*)

(**FREDDIE** *approaches the house. He calls out.*)

FREDDIE. Hello? (*no answer*) Charity?

(**CHARITY** *comes out.*)

CHARITY. Freddie, what are you doing here?

FREDDIE. I thought I'd come by to see you.

ESPERANZA. (*offstage*) ¡Caridad! (*Charity!*)

CHARITY. Sí, mamá.

(**ESPERANZA** *comes out.*)

Mamá, this is Freddie…

ESPERANZA. I know who it is. ¿Por qué lo invitaste aquí? (*Why did you invite him here?*)

CHARITY. I didn't invite him here.

FREDDIE. *Mucho gusto, señora. (It's a pleasure, ma'am.)*

(*He extends his hand but she doesn't take it.*)

ESPERANZA. Humph…

(*She enters the house.*)

CHARITY. You shouldn't have come here. I told you…

FREDDIE. Sorry, if I'm causing you trouble…

CHARITY. It's not you, it's her. She's old fashioned.

FREDDIE. I guess most parents are, aren't they?

CHARITY. I guess..

(silence)

FREDDIE. I haven't stopped thinking about you since the dance.

CHARITY. Really?

FREDDIE. You're even prettier during the day.

(She laughs.)

CHARITY. Stop.

FREDDIE. I sure wish I could kiss you.

CHARITY. Shhh.

*(**FAITH** sticks her head out of the door and signals for **CHARITY** to come inside. **ESPERANZA** calls out from inside.)*

ESPERANZA. *(offstage) ¡Caridad! (Charity!)*

CHARITY. I gotta go in. *(She heads in.)*

FREDDIE. When can I see you again?

*(**SILVESTRE** comes out.)*

SILVESTRE. *Caridad…* Your mother wants you to come inside.

*(**FREDDIE** goes to him.)*

FREDDIE. *Buenas tardes, Señor Morales. (Good afternoon, Mr. Morales.)*

SILVESTRE. *Buenas tardes.* You're Federico. Aren't you Pablo's son?

FREDDIE. Yes, sir.

SILVESTRE. I knew your father. We worked on the same crew in the mine.

FREDDIE. Yes, I remember. He liked you very much. He liked what you were trying to do for the men at the mine.

ESPERANZA. *(offstage)* *¡Caridad!*

SILVESTRE. *Caridad, m'ija,* you have to come in. *(Charity, my daughter.)*

CHARITY. *Sí, papá. (Yes, father.)*

SILVESTRE. *Buenas tardes.*

>   (**SILVESTRE** *enters the house.*)

FREDDIE. Will you meet me somewhere? I mean, just to talk and get to know each other better?

CHARITY. I don't know. Bye.

>   (**FREDDIE** *leaves and* **CHARITY** *turns on the radio. Carmen Miranda sings five lines from "I, yi, yi, yi, yi."* Lights change and* **CHARITY** *dreams she is Carmen Miranda.*)

>   (**FAITH** *and* **ELENA** *enter and join in for another five lines.**)

>   (**CHARITY** *sings four lines alone.**)

>   (**ESPERANZA** *enters and turns off the radio.*)

---

* Please see Music Use note on page 3

Scene Nine

(**RICARDO FLORES** *arrives at the Morales home with his fedora hat in his hand.* **ESPERANZA** *does not look happy. The girls sit at the table.*)

RICARDO FLORES. *Buenas tardes, señora. (Good afternoon, ma'am.)*

ESPERANZA. *Buenas tardes. Pásele. Siéntese. (Good afternoon. Come in. Sit down.)*

(*He sits.*)

RICARDO FLORES. *Qué hijas tan talentosas tiene, señora.* What talented daughters you have, *señora.*

ESPERANZA. Humph… Cleaning and cooking is a talent, too. They should be more talented at that.

RICARDO FLORES. Oh, yes, it definitely is, *señora.* My mother, may she be with God in heaven, used to say that cleanliness is next to Godliness.

ESPERANZA. *¿De veras? (Really?)* So, why aren't you married to a woman who is Godly?

RICARDO FLORES. Me, oh, *señora,* God has given me a different path.

ESPERANZA. Which is?

RICARDO FLORES. Which is to be able to recognize the talents that God has given to others and to give those people the opportunity to help themselves, become successful and, in turn, help their loved ones.

ESPERANZA. Humph…

RICARDO FLORES. Let me tell you a story about a young man I met one day in a small town not too far from here. I stopped by a small restaurant to eat and there was a young man singing who had a beautiful voice and I thought that God must have wanted me to hear this young man sing. You know what I did?

GIRLS. (*engrossed*) What?

RICARDO FLORES. I took that boy under my wing, took him to Phoenix, then to *Los Angeles* and do you know who that young boy is?

GIRLS. Who?

RICARDO FLORES. Frankie Palomar...

CHARITY. The Frankie Palomar?

RICARDO FLORES. *Sí.* Your daughters are very talented, señora, and there is an amateur hour down at the radio station...

GIRLS. *¡Sí, mamá!* Please! Let us go, *mamá!*

ESPERANZA. *¡Cállense! (Quiet!)* You're not going! What will people think? I won't have my daughters singing on the radio so that everybody can hear their silliness. Absolutely not!

GIRLS. But, *mamá!*

ESPERANZA. Stop! I said "no" and it is "no!" *(She looks at* **RICARDO FLORES**.*)* And as for you Mr. Flores or Flowers or whatever your name is, I suggest you go sell your nonsense to somebody who doesn't care about the upbringing of their daughters and maybe you can marry one of them while you're at it.

(She hands him his hat.)

RICARDO FLORES. But...

ESPERANZA. Goodbye!

*(***RICARDO FLORES***, looking like he doesn't know what hit him, exits.* **ESPERANZA** *looks at the girls.)*

I don't want to hear another word about this. *(She exits.)*

*(***FAITH** *looks at* **CHARITY** *and* **ELENA**.*)*

FAITH. I don't know about you, but I'm going to the amateur hour.

CHARITY. What? You can't.

FAITH. Yes, I can!

ELENA. But...

FAITH. And you better be quiet or I'll tell all your friends at school that you fart in your sleep.

(**ELENA** *starts to cry.*)

ELENA. ¡Mamá! ¡Mamá!

(**CHARITY** *covers* **ELENA**'s *mouth with her hand.*)

CHARITY. Faith, don't do it. Mom will never forgive you.

FAITH. And?

(**ELENA** *can't breathe.*)

CHARITY. And when she finds out, she'll hit you, she'll punish you forever.

FAITH. I don't care. We're always punished anyway. I'm used to it. I'm tired of never having anything.

(**ESPERANZA** *enters.* **CHARITY** *let's go of* **ELENA**, *she breaths and runs to* **ESPERANZA**.)

ELENA. *Mamá*, Faith's going to tell my friends that I fart in my sleep. (**ELENA** *cries.*)

ESPERANZA. What am I going to do with you, Fe? Why can't you behave? All I want for you is to be good girls and obey me. When you have your own children, you'll understand and you will do the same.

FAITH. No, we won't!

ESPERANZA. What?

FAITH. We won't!

(**FAITH** *exits and runs to the balcony.* **ELENA** *looks at* **CHARITY**. *She can't lie.*)

CHARITY. We don't want to be like you. We never want to be like you. We hate the way you are.

(**ESPERANZA** *looks at* **CHARITY** *and* **ELENA**, *she sits, she cries.*)

ELENA. *No, mamacita, no llores.* (*No, don't cry, little mother.*) Don't cry…

CHARITY. I'm sorry, Mom… But, you asked.

(**FAITH** *makes her way to the swing. She sings three lines from "Moonlight Serenade."**)*

Scene Ten

(At the kitchen table **ESPERANZA** *talks to* **SILVESTRE**. *She has a letter in her hand.* **LUPE** *is nearby.)*

SILVESTRE. She's your mother, you have to go…

ESPERANZA. How can I leave? What about the girls?

SILVESTRE. I'll take care of them.

ESPERANZA. How? You are always at the mine. They need someone to be watching them.

LUPE. They're all grown up, comadre. They know how to cook and clean.

SILVESTRE. *¿Ya ves? (You see?)*

ESPERANZA. We don't have the money…

SILVESTRE. I'll get the money. You have to see your mother, ask for forgiveness before she dies.

LUPE. I'll help out. I'll come by every day and make sure they are okay.

ESPERANZA. *¿De veras? (Really?)* Thank you, *comadre*.

(She waves her off.)

LUPE. *No hay de que… (It's nothing…)*

ESPERANZA. I have to get everything ready.

(Lights up on the radio:)

FDR. Yesterday, 7 December 1941 – a date which will live in infamy – the United States of America was suddenly and deliberately attacked by naval and air forces of the Empire of Japan.

I ask that the Congress declare that since the unprovoked and dastardly attack by Japan on Sunday, 7 December, a state of war has existed between the United States and the Japanese Empire.

*(*ESPERANZA, SILVESTRE *and* LUPE *embrace.* CHARITY *and* ELENA *join* FAITH *on the swing as they sing five lines from "Moonlight Serenade."**)*

End of Act One

---

*Please see Music Use note on page 3

ACT TWO

Scene One

(**CHARITY** and **FAITH** are doing **ELENA**'s hair and makeup. Their braids are gone and replaced with pompadours and red lipstick. The Andrews Sisters sing "Shoo, shoo, baby" on the radio.* The girls sing along and dance. The house is a mess.)

(The song continues as **LUPE** enters and sees the **GIRLS** singing and dancing.** At first she disapproves. But, by the end she is enjoying the song and dancing, too. When the girls see her, they laugh. **LUPE** is embarrassed.)

LUPE. Bueno, I have to go. Your papá is out at one of those meetings again. There's beans and tortillas on the stove.

CHARITY. Elena can't eat beans.

(**ELENA** frowns.)

FAITH. Because she farts in her sleep.

(They laugh.)

LUPE. ¿A poco eres pedorrera, hija? (Don't tell me you're a farter, daughter?) Me too. Don't worry, when you get older... people get used to it.

(She laughs and exits. **CHARITY** is busy putting stamps into a war bonds stamp book. **FAITH** is putting makeup on **ELENA**.)

---

* Please see Music Use note on page 3
** Please see Music Use note on page 3

(FDR speech about the war – July 28, 1943. Audio on radio:)

FDR. The next time anyone says to you that this war is "in the bag," or says (and) "it's all over but the shouting," you should ask him these questions: "Are you working full time on your job?" "Are you growing all the food you can?" "Are you buying your limit of war bonds?" "Are you loyally and cheerfully cooperating with your Government in preventing inflation and profiteering, and in making rationing work with fairness to all?"

CHARITY. There, I need ten more stamps and I can buy a war bond and support President Roosevelt and our boys!

*(**ELENA** and **FAITH** rolls their eyes.)*

Scene Two

*(**SILVESTRE** is talking to his fellow miners.)*

SILVESTRE. We have worked in this mine for years with no protection, no safeguards. We work the most dangerous jobs and have risked our lives and we work as hard, if not harder than the Anglo workers. Why do we only make half of what they make? Because we are *mexicanos?* Because our skin is brown and our hair is black? Because we are poor? Why can our boys go to fight for their country but they are not good enough to earn what the Anglo workers make for the same job working in the mine? God put us all on this earth and we are all God's children. Believe me when I tell you that God, yes, God himself, is on our side.

Scene Three

(**FREDDIE**, *in a military uniform, and* **CHARITY** *are on the swing.* **ELENA** *is chaperoning from afar.*)

FREDDIE. Thanks for answering my letters.

CHARITY. Oh, it's the least I can do for our boys.

FREDDIE. Our boys? You mean, I wasn't the only one?

CHARITY. Oh, yes, I mean, it's just what we say: "It's the least we can do for our boys."

(*They laugh.*)

FREDDIE. Oh…

CHARITY. Freddie, have I told you how much I admire you?

(*He smiles.*)

FREDDIE. Do you really?

CHARITY. Uh huh. I mean, I know you got drafted, but still, what you're doing for our country, our freedom, our liberty… Gee…

FREDDIE. Well, I hope I can make you proud.

CHARITY. I'm already proud.

FREDDIE. I mean, prouder.

CHARITY. You will.

(*silence*)

FREDDIE. Your Mom still in Mexico?

CHARITY. Yeah. Her Mom died.

FREDDIE. Oh, I'm sorry to hear that.

CHARITY. Me too. We never met our grandparents because we could never afford to go to *México*.

FREDDIE. Yeah, I've never been there either. Shoot, going to boot camp was the first time I ever left this town. There's a whole world out there, Charity.

CHARITY. Gee, I wish I could see it.

ELENA. (*mocking* **CHARITY**) "Gee, I wish I could see it."

CHARITY. Why don't you get lost?

ELENA. Because you're not supposed to be alone with a boy and you know it.

CHARITY. I'm not alone. You're here, you pest.

*(**ELENA** buzzes like an insect.)*

ELENA. Bzzzzzz...

*(**CHARITY** ignores her.)*

CHARITY. My Mom will be back soon and, well, things will be the way they used to be.

FREDDIE. I like your mom.

CHARITY. You do?

FREDDIE. Yes, because she helped my mom when my dad died in the mine. We had no food, no money and your mom would come over and bring us beans and tortillas. I was so hungry those beans and tortillas were delicious. I promised I'd never complain about eating beans and tortillas again.

ELENA. I love beans...

CHARITY. We know! Hey, Freddie, you wanna know something about Elena?

ELENA. No! Okay, I'm sorry, I'm sorry!

CHARITY. Then, amscray!

ELENA. What?

CHARITY. Scram!

ELENA. Okay!

(She crosses her arms and leaves.)

CHARITY. I never knew my mother did that.

FREDDIE. Yup, and your mom even gave my mom a little money...

CHARITY. That's hard to believe.

FREDDIE. Maybe it is. But, it's true and I'll never forget it. You know what else I'll never forget? The time you shared your lunch with me because you knew I didn't have any. This whole town knew that we were hungry and everybody was kind...

CHARITY. Well, I'm glad to know my mom was nice to someone.

FREDDIE. Don't be so hard on your mom. You know, sometimes, parents love us so much, they can't let go.

(They sit on that thought for a moment.)

Hey, did you know Eleanor Roosevelt visited the Japs at the Gila River Camp?

CHARITY. She did? Why would she visit the Japs?

FREDDIE. Oh, I don't know. Maybe she feels sorry for them...

CHARITY. How could she feel sorry for them?

FREDDIE. The people in the camps didn't kill anyone... Some of them are as American as you and me, Charity. Our parents are from Mexico and their parents are from Japan, but... I don't know, I don't like to think about them in those camps.

CHARITY. What? What do you mean?

(He sees she's upset and skips the subject.)

FREDDIE. Ah, nothing. I think too much sometimes. *(silence)* Did you hear about Bobby Sánchez?

CHARITY. Of course, everybody in town knows. I feel so bad for his mother.

FREDDIE. So do I. I went to see her as soon as I got back. I really think it hurt her to see me, you know... still alive. I left as soon as I could.

CHARITY. Poor *Señora Sánchez...*

FREDDIE. I was thinking... I mean, I like you so much, Charity. The whole time I was in boot camp, the thought of you was what kept me going and...

CHARITY. Oh, I thought about you every second of every minute of every hour of every day...

FREDDIE. I know. *(He stops. He takes her aside.)* I've never said this to anyone...

CHARITY. Yes?

FREDDIE. I don't want to go to war. I'm… I don't want to die.

CHARITY. What?

(He sees the confusion in her face.)

FREDDIE. I feel like such a sap. But, would it be so bad if I didn't go? I mean, I'm not a conscientious objector, but I could say I am and you and me could…

CHARITY. Freddie, what are you saying? You have to go. Remember what President Roosevelt said "The only thing we have to fear, is fear itself." You have to fight for our country. You have to be brave…

FREDDIE. But, I'm not…

CHARITY. But, you have to be. You have to. I'll write to you every day and I'll wait for you and…

FREDDIE. …will you pray for me?

CHARITY. Of course, I will.

(They embrace, they kiss. **CHARLIE** *arrives.)*

CHARLIE. Hey, guys and dolls. What's the news?

FREDDIE. Hey, Charlie…

CHARLIE. Freddie, you are sure looking sharp in your uniform. If it weren't for my bum leg, I'd be out there fighting right next to you. I'd love to kill me some of them good for nothing Japs…

CHARITY. What's wrong with your leg, Charlie?

CHARLIE. Ah, I got hurt in the mine a while back and, well, it's never been the same.

CHARITY. Oh…

*(***ELENA*** enters. ***CHARLIE*** changes the subject.)*

CHARLIE. Hey, Charity, is your mom still in Mexico?

CHARITY. Yes.

CHARLIE. Happy days are here again!

CHARITY. But, she'll be back soon. Her Mom passed away.

CHARLIE. Oh, *qué gacho. (too bad) (He crosses himself.) Que en paz descanse… (May she rest in peace…)*

(ELENA *giggles at* CHARLIE's *shenanigans. He clears his throat.*)

Is Faith home?

CHARITY. Yes. (*She calls out:*) Faith!

(FAITH *comes out of the house wearing red lipstick and a slinky dress.*)

FREDDIE. Well, look who looks like a movie star.

FAITH. (*to* CHARITY) How's this for the amateur hour?

CHARITY. They're not going to see you…

FAITH. Yes, Mr. Flores told me there's a live audience. I'm meeting him later so he can take a look and listen to my song.

CHARLIE. I think you look swell! (*He whistles.*) Nice get-up. Nice chassis!

FAITH. What's whippersnapper doing here?

(ELENA *giggles again.*)

CHARLIE. I came to see my doll.

FAITH. Who, Elena?

CHARLIE/ELENA. No!

(FAITH *pulls out a cigarette. They all look at her in shock.*)

FAITH. Well, does anybody have a light?

(FREDDIE *pulls out some matches.* CHARLIE *takes them and lights* FAITH's *cigarette.*)

CHARLIE. Here, I'll light your cig.

FAITH. Thanks…

CHARLIE. Hey, Faith, what do you say Freddie and Charity and me and you ankle on down to the show. There's a new James Cagney movie, "Yankee Doodle Dandee." (*imitating James Cagney:*) "Mmmmm, you dirty rat…"

(ELENA *giggles.*)

FAITH. Are you paying? We don't have any money.

CHARLIE. (*sheepishly*) Well, no, I ain't got no dough…

FAITH. Forget it Charlie. It's not personal. I just like 'em a little taller, a little smarter and a little older.

CHARLIE. Gee, Faith, do you have to let a fella down so hard? I'm almost eighteen. What do I have to do?

*(**ELENA** giggles again and **CHARLIE** notices her this time.)*

(Music: The Andrew's Sisters' "I Want To Be Loved.'")

*(**FAITH** and **CHARITY** alternate singing fourteen lines from "I Wanna Be Loved," sometimes singing together.*)*

*(**CHARITY** and **FREDDIE** kiss and leave hand in hand. **FAITH** leaves to see **RICARDO FLORES**. **CHARLIE** and **ELENA** stand alone, she gives him a kiss on the cheek. He looks at **ELENA** in a different way. As **ELENA** runs inside, she farts.)*

(Sound cue: fart sound)

Scene Four

(As **CHARLIE** *sits on the swing alone, humming "I
Wanna Be Loved" quietly.** **SILVESTRE** *arrives, dirty
and tired from working in the mine.)*

CHARLIE. *(all Eddie Haskell-ish) Buenas noches,* Mr. Morales.
(Good evening,) (He extends his hand.)

SILVESTRE. *Buenas noches,* Carlos.

CHARLIE. I just came by to see if Mrs. Morales was back.
I heard about her mother. I wanted to give her my
condolences.

SILVESTRE. That's very nice of you...

CHARLIE. It's the least I can do. After all, she is a pillar of
our town. Everyone knows she's a good samaritan. My
mother says she helped her bring me into the world.
She's like a second mother to me.

SILVESTRE. Is that right?

CHARLIE. Yes, sir.

*(***SILVESTRE** *sits, exhausted physically and mentally.)*

How did the meeting go today, sir? I was very torn
between going there and coming to express my
sorrow...

SILVESTRE. Not too good.

CHARLIE. No? *(silence)* My pops... He says the company will
never let us organize. He says that we should be happy
we have jobs in the mine.

SILVESTRE. I understand. But, all men were created equal
in God's eyes and we can't stand by and do nothing
when we see the injustices that go on in the mine. You
see, in the end, Carlos, all we have is our dignity and
sometimes we have to fight for it.

CHARLIE. Yes, sir. I'll keep that in mind. Well, I better get
going. *Buenas noches. (Good night.)*

SILVESTRE. *Buenas noches...*

---

* Please see Music Use Note on page 3

(**CHARLIE** *leaves.* **SILVESTRE** *sits on the swing and hums an old Mexican song as he looks out into the distance.* **CHARITY** *and* **ELENA** *come out and join him. They sing "Cuatro Milpas" by Aristeo Silvas Antúnez.**)

(*As they sing,* **FAITH** *gets ready to sneak out of the house to go see* **RICARDO FLORES**.)

---

* Please see Music Use Note on page 3

Scene Five

(**FAITH** *is with* **RICARDO FLORES** *at the radio station.*)

RICARDO FLORES. I haven't seen anyone as pretty since I saw Betty Grable performing at the Hollywood Canteen where she auctioned off her stockings for one thousand dollars to support the war.

(**FAITH***'s taking it all in.*)

Let's see… Turn around. (*He whistles.*) You know, this amateur hour could be your big break. That's how Frank Sinatra was discovered and I already told you about Frankie Palomar…

FAITH. Yes. Do you really think…

RICARDO FLORES. You got the looks and you got the talent. If you win who knows what can happen. A recording contract maybe or I have a friend who has a club in L.A.

FAITH. Honestly, Mr. Flores?

RICARDO FLORES. Ricky, to you. Would I lie to you? I know what it is to have a dream. I had dreams, too, when I was young… I'm just surprised your mother changed her mind…

(*She cuts him off.*)

FAITH. Do you like the song I chose?

RICARDO FLORES. "I Wanna Be Loved"? It's perfect and… very sexy.

(**FAITH** *feels uncomfortable.*)

FAITH. I gotta go.

RICARDO FLORES. Okay, see you on Saturday. And remember, Faith, not everybody's dreams come true. But, I'm gonna make sure yours do.

FAITH. Thank you, Mr. Flowers. See you then. (*She exits.*)

*(Lights change. **RICARDO FLORES** remembers… Many years earlier, **RICARDO FLORES** is crooning "Amapola" – horribly.*)*

(The audience boos.)

*(**RICARDO FLORES** continues singing.*)*

(The audience boos him off the stage. Lights change. Back to present. He leaves the station.)

---

* Please see Music Use Note on page 3

Scene Six

(As **RICARDO FLORES** *leaves the station he sees* **LUPE** *walking down the street.)*

RICARDO FLORES. *Buenas noches, señora. (Good evening, ma'am.)*

LUPE. *Buenas.*

RICARDO FLORES. You look as lovely as ever.

(She giggles.)

LUPE. *Ay, Señor Flores.*

RICARDO FLORES. Are you going to come to the amateur hour at the radio station next week?

LUPE. Of course. I wouldn't miss it.

RICARDO FLORES. Are you sure you can't sing? You look to me like a woman of many talents.

LUPE. *Ay, Mr. Flores,* the truth is that when I was young I used to dream of so many things. Of being a singer, of being a dancer, of being rich, *imagínate. (imagine that)* Silly dreams.

RICARDO FLORES. No, not silly, *señora.* I don't think we ever stop dreaming. Sometimes life makes us dream smaller, but we never stop dreaming. We just dream for something different. Take me, for instance. My dream is to be able to help young talented people and make their dreams come true...

LUPE. That is so kind of you.

RICARDO FLORES. Yes, well...

LUPE. Don't you ever dream of meeting the right woman and falling in love.

RICARDO FLORES. Yes, of course... But, it hasn't happened yet, and, who knows if it ever will.

LUPE. A handsome, young man like you must have lots of female admirers.

RICARDO FLORES. No. *(He shakes his head.)* The ones I like are usually taken.

*(***LUPE*** blushes.)*

Señora Lupe...

LUPE. Yes.

RICARDO FLORES. You know where I live, don't you?

LUPE. Yes.

RICARDO FLORES. Would you come over one of these days and cook me a meal? I would love a home cooked meal for once.

LUPE. Come over? But, if people see me...

RICARDO FLORES. Single men hire women to cook and clean for them all the time. Why would people think anything? How about Saturday after the amateur hour?

LUPE. Alright.

RICARDO FLORES. I will be forever grateful. *(He kisses her cheek.) Bueno, (Well,)* I have to go... *Adiós. (Goodbye.)*

(She touches the cheek he kissed.)

LUPE. *Adiós...*

(He leaves. **LUPE** *exits, out of breath.)*

Scene Seven

(**CHARITY** and **ELENA** are preparing for **SILVESTRE** to get home with a bucket of water, towels, etc.)

CHARITY. I hope she gets home before Dad does.

ELENA. What do we say if she doesn't?

CHARITY. Nothing. Maybe he won't ask.

ELENA. But, what if…

(**SILVESTRE** arrives stage left.)

CHARITY. Shhh… Hi, Dad.

ELENA. Hola, papá. (Hello, Dad.)

CHARITY. Are you tired? Here, let us soak your feet.

(They remove his shoes and socks. **SILVESTRE** looks around for **FAITH**. They try to distract him.)

ELENA. Papá…

SILVESTRE. ¿Qué? (What?)

(**ELENA** doesn't know what to say.)

CHARITY. Was mamá pretty when she was young?

SILVESTRE. O, tu mamá estaba bien bonita. (Oh, your mother was very pretty.) I mean, she's still pretty. But, back then…

CHARITY. Prettier than us, papá?

SILVESTRE. Pues… almost, I think. And she was determined to get what she wanted. I didn't know what hit me!

CHARITY. That doesn't surprise me.

ELENA. Did you really meet in church, papá?

(He doesn't know what to say.)

SILVESTRE. Is that what your mother told you?

ELENA. Yes, but she didn't say how.

SILVESTRE. Well, she would come to church every day for communion. There was mass three times a day and there she was, every day.

CHARITY. Was she that religious?

ELENA. Not anymore…

SILVESTRE. It was a different time, then. The Revolution… Your *mamá* lost her grandmother and her sister.

ELENA. And you, *papá?*

SILVESTRE. Me? I wanted to get as far away from the violence and the hunger. Back then we were so hungry, one time I ate dead flies.

GIRLS. Eww…

SILVESTRE. I was starving and they were delicious.

GIRLS. Ugh!

(He laughs.)

SILVESTRE. Your mother said, *vámonos pa'l norte (let's go north)* and that's what we did.

(They hug him.)

Ay, mis muchachitas. (Oh, my little girls.)

*(**FAITH** enters, wearing lipstick and slinky dress. **SILVESTRE** looks at her.)*

Fe, ¿dónde andabas, m'ija? (Faith, where were you, my daughter?"

FAITH. Oh, I just went out to see some friends.

SILVESTRE. You know your mother wouldn't let you dress like that.

FAITH. She won't let me do anything, Dad.

(He smiles.)

SILVESTRE. She wants you to be nice girls. I do too. We want you to go to school, get good grades, graduate, meet nice men, have good families.

FAITH. Not me. I'm not getting married and having children. I'm gonna be a singer.

SILVESTRE. What? No, *m'ija*, I want to walk each one of you down the aisle. That's why your mom is strict and that's what I work so hard for.

*(**ELENA** interrupts.)*

ELENA. I heard some of the men talking at the store, *papá*. They said you're going to get in trouble because you want *pleito. (trouble)*

(He laughs.)

SILVESTRE. I don't want trouble. Is that what they said?

(She starts to cry.)

ELENA. Yes. What will they do to you, *papá?* Will they kill you?

(He laughs.)

SILVESTRE. No, they won't kill me. They may run me out of town, but they won't kill me.

ELENA. *No, papá!* What will we do without you and without *mamá?*

SILVESTRE. *Ya, ya...* Nothing is going to happen to me. *Mamá* will be back. She's coming back on Saturday.

FAITH. What?

SILVESTRE. Yes, I got a telegram. She's coming home.

(They exit. On the radio:)

FDR. Mr. Chief Justice, Mr. Vice President, my friends, you will understand and, I believe, agree with my wish that the form of this inauguration be simple and its words brief. I remember that my old schoolmaster, Dr. Peabody, said, in days that seemed to us then to be secure and untroubled: "Things in life will not always run smoothly. Sometimes we will be rising toward the heights – then all will seem to reverse itself and start downward.

Scene Eight

RICARDO FLORES. *Les habla su servidor, Ricardo Flores.* I am Ricardo Flores, but for those of you who prefer the American language, you can call me Ricky Flowers. Today is Saturday and you all know what that means. It's the Amatuer Hour this evening at 5 o'clock.

(**FAITH** *is getting ready for the amateur hour. She has on a sexy dress and* **CHARITY** *is combing her hair while* **FAITH** *puts on red lipstick.*)

CHARITY. Faith, Mom's coming home. If she finds out...

FAITH. How's she gonna find out? *(She looks at* **ELENA.***)* Remember, if you say anything..

ELENA. I won't...

CHARITY. People will tell her.

FAITH. By that time, it'll all be over. Hurry, I gotta go before she gets here.

CHARITY. Hold on. I just need to put some more pins in...

(**ESPERANZA** *enters with suitcase and coat and sees* **FAITH** *dressed in the slinky dress and wearing lipstick. She stops, looks at her and* **ELENA** *blurts out.*)

ELENA. She's going to sing at the Amateur Hour...

(**ESPERANZA** *puts her suitcase down and looks at* **FAITH.***)*

ESPERANZA. *¿Es cierto, Fe? (Is it true, Faith?)*

FAITH. Yes, I am.

(She starts gathering her things.)

ESPERANZA. *¡No vas, Fe! (You're not going, Faith!)*

FAITH. Yes, I am going!

ESPERANZA. *¡No vas! (You won't go!)*

FAITH. *¡Sí voy! (I'm going!)* I'm sick and tired of you treating me like a child. I can't do anything, can't go anywhere. What do you think I'm gonna do, Mom, become a street walker? A *puta*? *(whore)* Why did you have to come back? We were so happy without you.

ESPERANZA. *¡Cállate la boca, Fe!* (Shut your mouth, Faith!)

FAITH. *¡Me callo, nada!* (I won't shut up!)

ESPERANZA. *¡Te digo que te calles!* (I said shut up!)

FAITH. *¡No!*

(**ESPERANZA** *goes to a shelf and grabs a bottle of poison.*)

ESPERANZA. *¡Cállate o me tomo este veneno!* (Shut up or I'll drink this poison!) I'll kill myself!

(**CHARITY** *and* **ELENA** *fall to their knees.*)

CHARITY/ELENA. *¡No! ¡Mamacita por favor!* (No! Little mother, please!)

ESPERANZA. *Sí, me lo voy a tomar.* (I will drink it.) I'd rather die than to have a daughter that disobeys me.

(**FAITH** *stands with her arms crossed.*)

FAITH. What are you waiting for? Drink it..

CHARITY. Faith, please be quiet.

FAITH. Stupids. Do you really think she's gonna drink it? She's not gonna drink rat poison.

ELENA. *¡Mamacita, no mamacita!* (Little mother, no, little mother!)

ESPERANZA. You don't believe that I'll drink it? That I'll kill myself because of you?

FAITH. No, I don't!

ESPERANZA. Yes, I will.

FAITH. No, you won't!

(**SILVESTRE** *enters and* **ESPERANZA** *slaps* **FAITH**.)

SILVESTRE. *¿Qué pasa?* (What's going on?)

ESPERANZA. *¡Ay, Silvestre, esta muchacha me va matar!* (Oh, Silvestre, this girl is going to kill me!) She wants to sing on the radio like a street walker.

(*He goes to* **FAITH**.)

SILVESTRE. *A ver, dime. (Let's see, tell me.)*

(**FAITH** *cries.*)

CHARITY. Ricardo Flores…

SILVESTRE. Who?

ELENA. Ricardo Flores from the radio program.

CHARITY. He came and said that he wanted us to go to the amateur hour…

ELENA. Because he heard us sing at the talent contest at the dance…

CHARITY. And he thinks we are very talented…

ELENA. But, Mom, said "no" and we thought that was that, but Faith…

CHARITY. Well, she wanted to go Dad because she, I mean we… We love to sing and we just want to be like every other American girl.

(**SILVESTRE** *takes* **FAITH** *aside.*)

SILVESTRE. *Fe, hija, por favor. (Faith, my daughter, please.)* Don't do this to your mother. Please obey us. I know you are a good girl…

(**FAITH** *cries. He holds her.*)

FAITH. *(whispers)* I hate her, Dad. I hate her so much…

SILVESTRE. No, *hija. (daughter)* Please don't say that.

(**FAITH** *exits.*)

(*Music: "Moonlight Serenade".**)

(**FAITH** *sings the first four lines.**)

(**CHARITY** *sits in the livingroom.*)

(**FAITH, CHARITY,** *and* **ELENA** *sing the next three lines.**)

(**ESPERANZA** *goes to the swing.* **ELENA** *joins her.*)

(**FAITH, CHARITY,** *and* **ELENA** *sing the next two lines.**)

---

*Please see Music Use Note on page 3

(**RICARDO FLORES** *shows up with a coat and a suitcase. He helps* **FAITH** *into the coat, she picks up the suitcase and leaves with him.*)

(**LUPE** *is at* **RICARDO FLORES**' *holding warm tortillas wrapped in a kitchen towel.*)

LUPE. Hello? *Señor Flores?* Mr. Flowers?

(*She realizes he's not home. She leaves. Music out.*)

Scene Nine

ESPERANZA. All I ever wanted was for you to be good girls and your sister runs away. What do you think people are thinking of her? Of me?

(The girls are silent.)

They're thinking that I raised her wrong. That I didn't take care of her. What was I going to do? Let you do what you want? Wear lipstick, walk the streets, kiss boys, get into trouble? I know you like Marta's son, Freddie. I'm glad he went off to war before you...

*(**CHARITY** cries.)*

Ay, m'ija, don't worry. *(Oh, my daughter,)* You'll find a good man to marry. *Vas a ver... (You'll see...)*

CHARITY. But, I want to marry him.

ESPERANZA. No, you don't. He has no future. His family is poorer than we are. You don't have to marry a poor man.

CHARITY. Yes, I do.

ESPERANZA. What?

(She doesn't answer.)

ELENA. You might as well tell her. You know we can't lie.

ESPERANZA. Tell me what? *(She looks at **ELENA**.) Dime, Elena. (Tell me, Elena.)*

ELENA. She's e-x-p-e-c-t-i-n-g...

*(**CHARITY** looks at **ESPERANZA** sadly...)*

CHARITY. I'm sorry, Mom...

(Audio: announcement of the death of President Roosevelt)

RADIO VOICE. We interrupt this program to bring you a special news bulletin from CBS World News. A press association has just announced that President Roosevelt is dead. The president died of a cerebral hemorrhage. All we know so far is that the president died in Warm Springs, Georgia...

(sound fades)

Scene Ten

FAITH. Dear Dad, I want you to know that I'm alright. Please, don't worry about me. I'm in *Los Angeles* and I have a job. Mr. Flores is taking good care of me. And it's not what you think. Mr. Flores, I mean Ricky, he doesn't like me that way. He doesn't like any woman that way. I'm sorry for what I said about Mom. I didn't mean it and I'm sorry if I hurt you, Dad. Please give my love to Charity and Elena. I miss them so much. But, I'm happy, Dad. I love you. I'm sorry. Love, Faith.

Scene Eleven

(**ESPERANZA** and **SILVESTRE** are talking.)

ESPERANZA. I must have been crazy to leave the girls. You always at your meetings and Lupe with her sick husband and busy flirting with the men in town. *¿Qué chingados estaba pensando yo? (What the hell was I thinking?)*

SILVESTRE. That's enough! Stop! She's not the first girl to get into trouble!

(**CHARITY** appears. Listening at the door.)

Don't make her feel worse than she does already. It's bad enough that we have to tell her...

ESPERANZA. How can we tell her, Silvestre? How can we tell her that Freddie is dead?

(They see **CHARITY**. She cries...)

CHARITY. No! No... (She runs to **SILVESTRE**'s arms.) No, papá, no...

(**ESPERANZA** and **SILVESTRE** hold **CHARITY** as she falls apart.)

Scene Twelve

(ELENA is on the swing. CHARLIE stands nearby. ELENA is all grown up.)

ELENA. My Dad went to find Faith in *Los Angeles.* She should be back soon. Are you gonna wait for her?

CHARLIE. Nah, she never liked me. She made it clear from the beginning.

ELENA. That's because the women in our family can't lie, no matter what.

CHARLIE. Is that right?

ELENA. Yup. It's been that way through the ages. I don't know why, but it's true.

(silence)

CHARLIE. How's Charity?

ELENA. How do you think she is? Awful! With Freddie dead and with her e-x-p-e... Well, you know...

CHARLIE. I know.

ELENA. I heard some ladies whispering about it at the store. I felt like busting them right in the kisser!

(CHARLIE laughs.)

CHARLIE. Don't tell me you're a troublemaker like your dad.

ELENA. You think my dad is a troublemaker?

CHARLIE. No... I mean I'm just saying...maybe he should mind his own business instead of trying to help everyone. I mean, he's a good guy and everything, but he's gonna make it worse for everyone.

ELENA. How?

CHARLIE. By going up against the bosses. The company, Elena... I mean, they own this town. The mine, the store, the houses, the hospital. They even own the... houses of ill repute.

ELENA. They do?

CHARLIE. Yes, they do. People have tried to do what your dad is doing before and they either land up dead or in jail.

ELENA. I don't want that to happen to my dad.

(She looks worried.)

CHARLIE. Hey, don't worry. I'm not trying to scare you or anything… *(silence)* So, you really can't lie, huh?

ELENA. No, I told you, none of us can.

CHARLIE. Do you like me?

(Silence. Then –)

ELENA. *(very softly)* Yes.

(He sits next to her on the swing.)

CHARLIE. I can't believe you've been around all this time and I never noticed how pretty you are…

(ELENA giggles. He takes her hand and they swing.)

Scene Thirteen

(FAITH *is in a sleazy L.A. night club singing a sexy version of "I Wanna Be Loved," with* RICARDO FLORES *watching nervously from the sidelines, smoking a cigarette.* FAITH *and* ELENA *sing the same song back home.**)

(FAITH *sings the first two lines.**)

(SILVESTRE *enters and sees* FAITH *singing.*)

(FAITH *continues singing two more lines.**)

(*Crossfade to:* ELENA *sings on the swing with* CHARLIE. CHARITY *sings alone in the house.* FAITH *sings in the club.*)

(FAITH, CHARITY, *and* ELENA *sing four lines of "I Wanma Be Loved" together.**)

(SILVESTRE *goes to* FAITH.)

SILVESTRE. *Fe…*

(*She is startled to hear his voice.*)

FAITH. Dad…

(*They embrace.*)

O, papá.

SILVESTRE. I came to take you home.

FAITH. I can't… I can't go home, Dad. Everything has changed. I've changed. The whole world has changed. Even if I went back… I know what people must be saying about me. I can't go back, Dad. I'm sorry…

---

*Please see Music Use Note on page 3

Scene Fourteen

(Music: "Amapola"*)

(SILVESTRE and ESPERANZA in the house.)

SILVESTRE. God is punishing us, Esperanza.

ESPERANZA. Don't say that, Silvestre. It isn't true.

SILVESTRE. It is true. He will never allow me to be happy in this life, Esperanza, never.

(She covers his mouth with her hand.)

ESPERANZA. Shhh... Don't...

SILVESTRE. We can pretend, Esperanza. We both know it's true... But, you were so beautiful and you pulled me... I could feel your gaze while I was giving mass, when I put the host in your mouth, when I confessed you, you pulled me away and I couldn't resist you...

---

*Please see Music Use Note on page 3

Scene Fifteen

(Music: Guitar plays "Valentina"*)

(Crossfade to: back in time. **YOUNG ESPERANZA** *is confessing, as in the prologue. The young priest is* **YOUNG SILVESTRE**.*)*

YOUNG ESPERANZA. Bless me father for I have sinned. It has been one day since my last confession.

YOUNG SILVESTRE. One day, my child?

YOUNG ESPERANZA. Yes, father.

YOUNG SILVESTRE. How much can you sin in one day?

YOUNG ESPERANZA. *(sigh)* Plenty. But, how can one control one's thoughts, one's imagination?

YOUNG SILVESTRE. I understand…

YOUNG ESPERANZA. *(whispers)* I can't stop thinking about the man I love. His eyes, his face, his hands, his body…

(YOUNG SILVESTRE *breathes hard. Clears his throat.)*

YOUNG SILVESTRE. You can't…

YOUNG ESPERANZA. Why not? He's a man and I'm a woman…

YOUNG SILVESTRE. It's a sin.

YOUNG ESPERANZA. No. To love is not a sin. Love cannot be a sin…

YOUNG SILVESTRE. You can't… I can't…

YOUNG ESPERANZA. Why not? You're a man…

YOUNG SILVESTRE. I can't… I made a promise…

YOUNG ESPERANZA. And I am a woman…

YOUNG SILVESTRE. …to God.

YOUNG ESPERANZA. Father Silvestre…

YOUNG SILVESTRE. Yes, my child?

YOUNG ESPERANZA. Do you love me?

YOUNG SILVESTRE. Yes, but…

*Please see Music Use Note on page 3

YOUNG ESPERANZA. I love you too…

YOUNG SILVESTRE. It's a sin…

YOUNG ESPERANZA. No! To love is not a sin! The sin is this wretched war that is destroying us all! The sin is the hunger that is killing us. It's a sin not to be able to walk down the street for fear of being hit by a bullet. It's a sin to have to walk past dead, rotting bodies with their intestines hanging out. To love is not a sin. It's a sin not to love. It's a sin not to be able to love the person who loves you.

(*YOUNG ESPERANZA* and *YOUNG SILVESTRE* *kiss.*)

Let's go. Far, far away from here. Let's go where nobody will know who we are or where we come from…

(*They embrace and hold on to each other for dear life. The run offstage.*)

Scene Sixteen

(Crossfade to: back to present)

ESPERANZA. You fell in love with me…

SILVESTRE. It wasn't love, *Esperanza.* It was lust. I was never yours…

(ESPERANZA cries.)

ESPERANZA. You didn't love me? You never loved me?

SILVESTRE. Of course, I love you and I love my daughters. But… *(He falls silent.)*

ESPERANZA. Say it…

SILVESTRE. Deep in my heart, I belong to God. To the promise I made so many years ago.

(ESPERANZA cries.)

ESPERANZA. Get out. Please get out of here and never come back. Go away. For your own good and for the good of our daughters. I will never be able to live with you. You coward. You were always a priest. You were never a man. You could never stand up to God.

(He tries to hold her.)

SILVESTRE. Esperanza…

(She pulls away.)

ESPERANZA. Go. Get out.

Scene Seventeen

(**SILVESTRE** *is talking to the miners.*)

SILVESTRE. We are the cheap labor that keeps this mine going. Without us, there is no mine, no production, no copper. The mine owners are getting richer because of our sweat, our labor… The rich get richer and the poor get poorer. And nothing will change until we speak up. Nothing will change until we stand up. Nothing will change until we go on strike!

(*Sound cue: a gunshot*)

CHARLIE. *Señor Silvestre,* you better run! They're coming after you. The police are going to arrest you. *¡Córrale! (Run!)*

(*Another shot is heard.*)

(*Lights up on* **ESPERANZA** *at the house.*)

ESPERANZA. *¡Silvestre!*

Scene Eighteen

(CHARLIE, ELENA and ESPERANZA.)

CHARLIE. He got away. They took him to the border and he got away. I don't think he'll be back for a while. He can't..

(ESPERANZA is numb.)

Señora, I couldn't go to the war because of my leg. But, I still have a job in the mine and I know Elena's only fifteen, but we love each other and I want to marry her...

(ESPERANZA doesn't answer respond.)

ELENA. *Mamá,* did you hear what Charlie said?

ESPERANZA. Yes, I heard.

VOICE OF PRESIDENT TRUMAN. Sixteen hours ago an American airplane dropped one bomb on Hiroshima and destroyed its usefulness to the enemy. That bomb had more power thantwenty thousand tons of TNT. It had more than two thousand times the blast power of the British "Grand Slam" which is the largest bomb ever yet used in the history of warfare.

Scene Nineteen

(Music: "Sentimental Journey")*

(FAITH reads a letter from CHARITY:)

CHARITY. Dear Sis, I miss you so much. I guess you know
about Freddie by now... He didn't want to go and
I... Can you believe I'm going to be a mother? Dad's
gone and Mom is trying to be nice, but I know she's
so ashamed. You know how people talk in this town...
I had to quit school and I don't even like going to the
store because... I just wanna curl up and die... I wish
you were here...

*(ESPERANZA reads a letter from FAITH. Lights up on
FAITH in Los Angeles.)*

(Sound: ocean waves)

FAITH. Dear Mom, I got a letter from Dad. He told me
that he had to go back to Mexico. I know you'll never
forgive me for what I did, but, if you ever can, I wish
you and my sisters would come to Los Angeles. I miss
you all so much. We can work and help each other.
Los Angeles is so big and so full of people. Nobody
cares about your past, whether you're rich or poor,
whether you're married or not. Everybody's too busy
living, Mom. And the ocean... the ocean is beautiful.
Please, Mom, think about it...

(sound out)

*(ESPERANZA and LUPE are sitting, drinking tequila
and smoking cigarettes.)*

LUPE. How can you let her get married? She's only fifteen
years old?

ESPERANZA. That's how old I was when I got married...

LUPE. I was fourteen. *Qué tonta...* (How dumb...)

(They sigh.)

*Please see Music Use Note on page 3

ESPERANZA. If I don't let her get married, she'll just do what the other two did.

LUPE. *Pues, sí… (Well, yes…)* Have you heard from Silvestre?

ESPERANZA. No, I won't hear from him…

LUPE. *Qué cabrón… (What an ass…)*

(*They sigh.*)

ESPERANZA. *Fe* says that *Los Angeles* is so big that nobody cares about your past. That's all I want, to be swept up in a wave and get lost in an ocean of people…

(*Sound: ocean waves…*)

Scene Twenty

(Music: "Sentimental Journey"*)

*(Lights up stage left. **FAITH** sings "Sentimental Journey" softly underneath scene.)*

*(Lights up on **CHARLIE** and **ELENA**. She is wearing a hat and has a bouquet in her hand as rice falls and they kiss. **CHARITY** has her baby in her arms.)*

CHARITY. Toss the bouquet!

*(She does and **LUPE** catches it. They all laugh. **ESPERANZA**, **CHARITY** say goodbye to **LUPE**.)*

LUPE. *Ay, comadre*, what am I going to do without you?

ESPERANZA. You know you can come and stay with us anytime.

LUPE. No, I can't. My Dora's coming home with the baby. Besides, there are too many men in *Los Angeles*. Who knows what I might do. But, write to me, okay?

ESPERANZA. Yes, I will.

*(They embrace. **ELENA** embraces **ESPERANZA**.)*

ELENA. I'm gonna miss you so much, Mom.

*(**ESPERANZA** embraces **ELENA**. **LUPE** takes **ESPERANZA** by the arm.)*

LUPE. *Comadre*, you should say something. Some words of wisdom, a *consejo*. *(advice)*

ESPERANZA. What should I say?

(Sound cue: Ancient Náhuatl drums and flutes)

*(**ESPERANZA** remembers the words of the elders that were shared with her so many years ago.)*

"Do not forget that you have come from someone; that you are descended from someone; that you were born by the grace of someone; that you are both the

---

*Please see Music Use Note on page 3

spine and the offspring of our ancestors; of those who came before us and of those who have gone on to the beyond." I wish you...the best.

(Lights up on FAITH *in Los Angeles, as* ESPERANZA *and* CHARITY *pick up their suitcases.)*

*(*FAITH, CHARITY, *and* ELENA *sing the ninth through twelfth lines of "Sentimental Journey."**)*

(Lights up SILVESTRE *dressed in priest vestments, talking to workers in México.)*

SILVESTRE. *En el nombre del padre, del hijo y del espiritu santo... (In the name of the Father, the Son, and the Holy Spirit...)*

*(*FAITH, CHARITY, *and* ELENA *sing the next four lines.*)*

*(*ESPERANZA, LUPE *and* CHARITY, *with the baby in her arms, exit.* ELENA *stands alone with* CHARLIE. *Lights fade to black.)*

End of Play

---

* Please see Music Use Note on page 3

Hope

Part II

(1960 – 1963)

HOPE: PART II OF A MEXICAN TRILOGY was first produced by the Latino Theater Company in Los Angeles, CA on October 28, 2011 at the Los Angeles Theatre Center. The performance was directed by Jose Luis Valenzuela, with sets by Francois-Pierre Couture, lights by Cameron Mock, costumes by Raquel Barreto, sound by John Zalewski, choreography by Urbanie Lucero, and music by Benjamin Taylor. The Production Stage Manager was Henry "Heno" Fernandez. The cast was as follows:

ELENA . . . . Dyana Ortelli
CARLOS . . . . Geoffrey Rivas
ENRIQUE . . . . .Sal Lopez
GINA . . . . .Esperanza America
BETTY . . . . Olivia Delgado
JOHNNY . . . . .Keith McDonald
BOBBY. . . . . .Dru Davis

CHARACTERS

ELENA – 30s, now married with children of her own, must face her husband's infidelity.

CARLOS (CHARLIE IN PART I) – is a good provider, but cheats on Elena and beats his children.

ENRIQUE – 40s, Carlos' friend and Elena's confidante, is married to a woman who suffers from depression.

GINA – 17, Elena's oldest daughter, is feisty and opinionated and bosses her younger siblings around.

BETTY – 16, is in love with President Kennedy and imagines having long conversations with him.

RUDY – 18, is in love with Gina.

JOHNNY – 15, thinks he's a ladies man.

BOBBY – 14, is kind and quiet. Carlos calls him a "Mama's boy."

MARI – 40s, suffers from melancholy, Enrique's wife.

JACK – President John F. Kennedy (can be played in silhouette).

FIDEL – Fidel Castro (can be played in silhouette).

SETTING

Phoenix, Arizona

The Garcia House

TIME

1960 – 1963

Prologue

(Thousands of images from the last century flash before us: the turn of the century, the revolution, the depression, WWI, WWII, the Korean War, Pancho Villa, Emiliano Zapata, FDR, Truman, Eisenhower, JFK, all in an instant and then it STOPS!)

(Footage: the inauguration of JFK, "My fellow Americans, ask not what your country can do for you. Ask what you can do for your country...")

(Music: "Dedicated To The One I Love"*)

(BETTY *sings the first line.*)*

(Lights up on **BETTY**, *15, wearing '50s clothes; a pencil skirt, sweater, flats.* **GINA**, *16,* **JOHNNY**, *14, and* **BOBBY**, *13, enter strolling to the music.)*

(BETTY *sings the second line.*)*

(GINA, JOHNNY, *and* **BOBBY** *underscore* **BETTY** *as she sings the next three lines.*)*

(The song ends and lights come up on:)

---

* Please see Music Use Note on page 3

ACT ONE

Scene One

(**BETTY** and **GINA**'s bedroom. **BETTY** lies on the bed hugging a pillow. **GINA** files her nails with big rollers in her hair.)

BETTY. Oh, he's so handsome... I love his smile. He's so smart. I could listen to him talk all day long. He's so brave, so courageous. He's so...manly...and...and... *(sigh)* so sexy...like a man, not a boy, but a man...

GINA. He is a man. Twice your age.

BETTY. I know, but I wanna marry him...

GINA. ...he's already married...

BETTY. ...but she's not right for him. He's so full of life and she's so...timid...frail... *(imitating)* her little voice... she's...

GINA. ...beautiful...

BETTY. She's not that beautiful...

GINA. You're the only person who doesn't think so. Everybody thinks she's beautiful, because she is...

BETTY. It doesn't matter. I wanna have his babies...

GINA. He already has a family, you can't.

BETTY. Why not? Give me one good reason.

GINA. One? Here's two. One – he doesn't even know you exist and two – he's the president of the United States of America.

(**BETTY**'s bubble is burst. She lies back on the bed.)

BETTY. But, I love him. Honestly, Gina, I think I'm in love with him.

GINA. You and every other woman.

(**BETTY** *sighs.*)

BETTY. I just love that we have a young, handsome president. He's so much better looking than that old what's his name.

GINA. Eisenhower.

BETTY. Yeah, Eisenhower. Ugh. *(pause)* I don't know, I just feel like everything is going to be okay. Like we are all going to live in peace and harmony.

(*Their mother yells from offstage, breaking their peace and harmony.*)

ELENA. *(offstage)* Gina? Betty? ¡Muchachas!

GINA/BETTY. Yeah?

ELENA. *(offstage)* Come and clean this kitchen. You made tortillas this morning and left a mess!

GINA. It was Betty!

BETTY. It was Gina!

ELENA. *(offstage)* ¡Muchachas! Cuantas veces les tengo que decir que limpien la cocina despues de hacer las tortillas. (Girls! How many times do I have to tell you to clean the kitchen after you make tortillas.) I am so tired of having to remind you girls…

(*Their mother's voice trails off as lights reveal* **ELENA**, *now in her 40s separating laundry,* **JOHNNY** *and* **BOBBY** *in their room.*)

(**BETTY** *and* **GINA** *sing the tenth through seventeenth lines of "Dedicated To The One I Love" as* **JOHNNY**, **BOBBY**, *and* **ELENA** *underscore.**)

Scene Two

(ELENA puts clothes into an electric roller washer. BOBBY, quiet and shy, watches ELENA, while JOHNNY, handsome and outgoing, combs his hair.)

BOBBY. Mom, do you really think we can send a man to the moon?

JOHNNY. Of course we can. Didn't you hear the president?

BOBBY. I'm asking Mom, not you.

(JOHNNY looks at ELENA.)

ELENA. If the president said we can...

JOHNNY. Told you...

ELENA. ...we can.

BOBBY. I hope it happens before 1970. I'll be an old man by then.

JOHNNY. John Fitzgerald Kennedy! JFK! The leader of the free world!

ELENA. He's a man of peace and that's all that counts. We don't want to lose any more boys to war like we did in World War II and Korea.

(silence)

BOBBY. I don't ever want to go to war.

ELENA. I don't want you to.

JOHNNY. I do. I mean, if we have to defend our country... Who knows, we might have to, and then what are you gonna do, pee your pants?

ELENA. Johnny stop.

BOBBY. Will we have to, Mom?

ELENA. No, President Kennedy is a good president... and he's so handsome.

(The boys give her a look.)

Well, he is!

BOBBY. Mom...does Dad know you think the president is handsome?

(She shrugs.)

ELENA. I doubt it.

JOHNNY. John Fitzgerald Kennedy…

BOBBY. JFK…

(Dog barks.)

ELENA. Did you remember to feed the dog?

*(**BOBBY** and **JOHNNY** look at each other and rush out.)*

That poor dog. It's going to starve to death…

(She picks up a white shirt and as she's about to put it in the washer, she notices there is lipstick on the collar. She looks closer. She smells the shirt. She sits on a chair feeling sick.)

*(**GINA** enters and sees **ELENA** holding the shirt. **ELENA** quickly shoves the shirt into the washer and exits. **GINA** goes to the washer takes out the shirt and sees the lipstick. She shoves it back into the washer. **BETTY** daydreams about President Kennedy in her room.)*

*(**BETTY** sings the first line from "Dedicated to the One I Love"*)*

(Footage: President Kennedy, the Cuban Missile Crisis, October 22, 1962)

JFK'S VOICE: Good evening, my fellow citizens:

This Government, as promised, has maintained the closest surveillance of the Soviet military buildup on the island of Cuba. Within the past week, unmistakable evidence has established the fact that a series of offensive missile sites is now in preparation on that imprisoned island. The purpose of these bases can be none other than to provide a nuclear strike capability against the Western Hemisphere.

(Air raid sirens sound.)

---

*Please see Music Use Note on page 3

Scene Three – The Weeping Willow

(GINA sits underneath the weeping willow tree, thinking alone.)

(Music: "Love Hurts"*)

(GINA sings the first seven lines.**)

(RUDY, young, handsome and love-struck, arrives.)

RUDY. Hi Gina.

GINA. *(unimpressed)* Hi.

RUDY. I waited for you yesterday.

GINA. I know, I'm sorry. I had homework. Had to study for a test.

RUDY. It's okay.

(He sits next to her.)

Can I hold your hand?

GINA. No!

RUDY. Why not?

GINA. Are you kidding me? We're on the brink of nuclear war. Don't you watch the news?

RUDY. Yeah, but… All I can think about is you and your smile and the way you wrinkle your forehead when you're mad, which is a lot of the time…

GINA. *(mad)* I'm not always mad!

RUDY. Okay, okay…

GINA. Betty and the boys say I'm mean…

RUDY. You're not mean.

GINA. Yes, I am.

RUDY. Okay, you're mean. *(RUDY looks at her.)* I think I love you…

(GINA frowns.)

---

* Please see Music Use Note on page 3
** Please see Music Use Note on page 3

GINA. You think?

RUDY. No, I mean, I do love you.

GINA. Well don't! I don't believe in love.

RUDY. You don't?

GINA. No. People fall in love and it lasts a little while and the next thing you know they have a whole bunch of kids and the husband is running around with other women and the wife just sits around crying, waiting for him to come back. It's crap, I hate it!

RUDY. It's not always that way…

GINA. Yes it is! Why do you think divorce rates are rising the way they are?

RUDY. I don't know.

GINA. Because people are unhappy and it's not like before when they had to stick it out and be miserable for the rest of their lives.

RUDY. It's not?

GINA. No, it's not. I wish my mom would divorce my dad.

RUDY. You do?

GINA. Yeah, but, she won't. She's too worried about what people will think. He leaves for weeks on end and she lets him come back every time. She's a doormat.

RUDY. She is?

GINA. Yeah…

　　(silence)

RUDY. I'm going away.

GINA. You are?

RUDY. I joined the Army.

GINA. You did?

RUDY. Yeah, before this whole nuclear missile stuff.

GINA. You never said you wanted to join the Army.

RUDY. Because I never did, but, well… I did. I mean, I felt like I should. My Dad signed up after Pearl Harbor and well I thought I should do my part, too. I didn't know I was signing up to die. It's just my luck.

(silence)

RUDY. My Dad was real happy. He says he's proud.

GINA. What about your mom?

RUDY. She pretended to be happy. She thinks the world is about to go up in smoke.

GINA. She's probably right.

RUDY. I know.

GINA. When do you leave?

RUDY. In two weeks. *(silence)* I was going to ask you...

GINA. Rudy, I already told you...

RUDY. Don't you even care for me a little bit?

GINA. Rudy, don't...

RUDY. Okay. *(pause)* Then, will you be my girl until I leave at least? I mean, we're headed for World War III and we're all gonna die anyway so you won't have to be my girl forever. You won't have to have a bunch of kids and wait for me to cheat on you and all that stuff. *(pause)* Please?

GINA. For two weeks?

(He looks at her hopefully.)

Yeah, okay...

(He puts his arm around her shoulder.)

Don't expect anything okay?

RUDY. I won't. *(He beams.)* Gina Garcia is my girlfriend...

(She gives him a look.)

...for two weeks.

*(**GINA** gets up.)*

GINA. See ya...

RUDY. See ya...

(She exits.)

(Music: "Love Hurts"*)

---

*Please see Music Use Note on page 3

(**RUDY** *sings the eighth through fourteenth lines.**)

(*He exits.*)

---

*Please see Music Use Note on page 3

Scene Four

(ENRIQUE, dark and handsome, and ELENA are in the kitchen. He drinks coffee as she dries dishes.)

ELENA. He's been gone for two days.

ENRIQUE. He's probably working, *el cabrón. (the ass)*

ELENA. I found lipstick on his shirt collar.

ENRIQUE. Are you sure it's lipstick?

ELENA. Yes, you can actually see the outline of the lips.

ENRIQUE. Oh... Well, I'm sure there's an explanation.

ELENA. Are you making excuses for him or trying to make me feel better?

ENRIQUE. *Pues... (Well...)* A little of both, I guess. I mean... *Sí, es un hijo de su, pero,* he's *my compadre, tu sabes. (Yeah, he's a son of a... but, he's my friend, you know.)*

ELENA. And what am I?

ENRIQUE. My *comadre,* but...

ELENA. But, what?

ENRIQUE. But, nothing, *hombre... (man...)* Why are you bringing me into this? I don't like being in the middle of you two. *Yo no me meto. (I don't butt in.)*

ELENA. I know there's someone and so do you. It's not the first time.

(He relents.)

ENRIQUE. *(gently)* And it probably won't be the last.

(She looks at him.)

Porque es un cabrón, hijo de la chingada. (Because he's a fuckin' asshole.)

ELENA. Shhh! The kids!

ENRIQUE. Sorry... But, you knew it when you married him, didn't you?

ELENA. I didn't know anything. I was fifteen years old.

(He looks at her.)

Tell me what to do?

ENRIQUE. What? Don't ask me for advice. *Yo que se? (What do I know?)*

ELENA. You're a man. You know how men think…

ENRIQUE. *Pues, (Well,)* I don't know… Tell him you saw it. Tell him you know.

ELENA. He'll just deny it.

ENRIQUE. Show it to him.

ELENA. He'll still deny it. He'll say he doesn't know where it came from. He'll say its not even his shirt. He'll deny it until I believe I'm the one who's making it up. You know it's true.

(ENRIQUE *gets serious.*)

ENRIQUE. Then leave him. You can leave him, Elena.

ELENA. And go where? To your house? Will *Mari* want me and my four kids in your house?

(ENRIQUE *doesn't answer.*)

That's what I thought.

ENRIQUE. You know she's not…well.

ELENA. I know…

(ENRIQUE *tries to make light of it.*)

ENRIQUE. My father always said, *"Cásate con una de México, m'ijo, esas son las buenas."* (Marry a girl from México, son. They are the best.) So, I follow his advice, go to *México,* marry the girl of my dreams and its been a nightmare ever since.

ELENA. That's not true. You two were very happy at the beginning.

ENRIQUE. In the beginning, maybe. I guess it didn't turn out the way we expected. (*He looks at* ELENA.) I guess, it never does, huh?

ELENA. I guess not.

(*They sit on that thought for a second.*)

ENRIQUE. It doesn't matter anyway. Didn't you hear JFK? The Russians are going to attack us any day. *Nos vamos a chicharronear.* We're gonna shrivel up and die

ELENA. I try not to show it to the kids, but I'm so scared. The other day a cloud covered the sun and I was sure it was an atomic cloud.

ENRIQUE. Everybody's like that. Walking around like we're doomed. Ah, what's the worse that can happen? *Nos queman y se acabó la canción. Ni modo. (They burn us up and it's over.)* It's bound to happen. The world can't go on forever.

ELENA. That's easy for you to say because you don't have kids. I want my kids to live their lives, get married, have kids.

ENRIQUE. *¿Pero por qué? ¡Es puro sufrir! ¡Pobresitos! (But why? It's nothing but suffering! Poor things!)* Why would you want that for them?

(They laugh. Then, ENRIQUE gets serious.)

Can't you go live with your mother?

ELENA. No, not after taking him back when she begged me not to. I don't want her to know. I'm embarrassed.

ENRIQUE. Men are stupid, Elena. We don't know anything, you know that. We just walk around looking for someone to…you know what. I don't know why, that's the way God made us, I guess.

ELENA. Gee, is that supposed to make me feel better?

ENRIQUE. I'm just trying to help you understand, *chingado. ("damn it")*

ELENA. You're not that way. *(pause)* Are you?

ENRIQUE. I don't know. I'm not like Carlos. But, I am a man…

(There is an uncomfortable silence between them. He gulps down his coffee.)

Bueno, (Well,) I gotta go.

ELENA. *Ándale pues. (Alright then.)* Say "hello" to *Mari* for me.

ENRIQUE. *Sí, hombre. (Sure.)*

   (He exits.)

   (Footage: Civil Defense, Duck and Cover video)

Scene Five

(GINA, BETTY, JOHNNY and BOBBY contemplate the atomic bomb.)

BETTY. The first thing that will happen is we'll see a bright flash and that's when...

BOBBY. We have to duck and cover.

JOHNNY. Maybe I'll duck. But, I'm not gonna cover.

BOBBY. You have to!

JOHNNY. Uh, uh. It'll mess up my hair.

BETTY. What do you do when we have duck and cover drills at school?

JOHNNY. I duck, but I don't cover.

(He chews gum and combs.)

BOBBY. You think its funny, I don't.

BETTY. I don't either. I have my whole life ahead of me.

JOHNNY. What, you think I wanna die? I don't. I just don't want to mess up my hair because there are a lot of young ladies who will be disappointed if I do.

BOBBY. If you die or mess up your hair?

JOHNNY. Both.

GINA. What young ladies?

JOHNNY. I have plenty of young ladies waiting in line.

GINA. Oh, God. Look who thinks he's God's gift to the female species.

BETTY. You can't have girlfriends. I can't have boyfriends and I'm older than you.

BOBBY. But, you're a girl.

GINA. And?

JOHNNY. And it's okay for me to have a girlfriend cuz I'm a boy and its not like I'm gonna get in trouble and have a baby and stuff.

BETTY. But, you can get a girl in trouble.

GINA. If you have sex with her.

BETTY. Gina!

GINA. The only way he can get a girl in trouble is if he has sex with her. That's a fact.

BOBBY. Ugh. I'm gonna throw-up.

BETTY. Remember Randy Bentley? He got a girl in trouble…

GINA. …because he had sex with her…

BETTY. …and his parents made him marry her and he was only seventeen years old. All his dreams, up in smoke…

(They sit on that thought for a second.)

BOBBY. Like an atomic bomb…

JOHNNY. I can't help it if I'm good looking.

GINA. Good looking? Says who?

JOHNNY. Mom. She says I get my good looks from Dad…

BOBBY. Yeah, she says Johnny takes after Dad and that I take after her side of the family because all the men in her family are good. And she says all the women in her family have big mouths like you.

(The girls look at BOBBY.)

Mom said it, not me.

(GINA looks at JOHNNY.)

GINA. You take after Dad?

JOHNNY. Yeah.

GINA. Ugh.

BETTY. What's so bad about taking after Dad?

GINA. Oh, please! Do I have to spell it out for you?

(Nobody speaks.)

BOBBY. What?

GINA. Don't act like you don't know. He cheats on Mom. He goes out with other women!

BETTY. He does not!

GINA. Oh, come on. He's been gone for days. Where do you think he is, Betty? Mom found lipstick on Dad's shirt. How do you think it got there, stupid?

BETTY. You're lying! You're always lying, Gina!

GINA. I'm not lying! Ask Mom!

BETTY. No! I'm not gonna ask her!

GINA. It's a fact, Betty! Facts are facts!

BETTY. You don't know anything!

GINA. I know you're stupid, that's what I know! Look at you! *(mocking* **BETTY***)* "We have to duck and cover." Don't you know that a nuclear bomb is going to fry everything and everybody in its path no matter what?

BETTY. You don't know.

GINA. Yes, I do.

BOBBY. You're lying.

GINA. Ever heard of Hiroshima?

BOBBY. No.

BETTY. I have.

GINA. What is it?

BETTY. It's a city where the atomic bomb went off.

JOHNNY. Yeah, like a big mushroom cloud grew in the sky. I know, we know.

GINA. *(to* **BOBBY***)* It's a city in Japan where we dropped an atomic bomb and over a hundred thousand people were burned to a crisp. Their skin was hanging off of their bodies in shreds like melted wax.

BETTY. Eww.

(**BOBBY** *looks scared.*)

BOBBY. Well, they probably didn't duck and cover like they were supposed to.

GINA. Yes, they did! And then we bombed Nagasaki and killed another seventy thousand people and then the Japanese surrendered. They say the stench of burned human flesh was unbearable. That's what's gonna happen to us.

BETTY. Stop trying to scare us, Gina!

GINA. I'm not trying to scare you. It's a fact. Ducking and
  covering won't protect anyone from an atomic bomb
  and Dad has sex with other women. Facts are facts!

BETTY. Shut up! Shut up!

  (BETTY *runs out of the room.*)

  (*Air raid sirens sound.*)

Scene Six

(The phone rings. **BETTY** *answers. A silhouette of* **JFK** *appears.)*

BETTY. Hello?

JACK. Hello, Betty. It's Jack…

BETTY. Oh, hello, Mr. President…

JACK. Please, call me Jack.

BETTY. Jack, I'm really scared. What is going on? Are we all going to die?

JACK. I'm doing my best to resolve the situation, Betty. But, Kruschev has an ego the size of the Milky Way…

BETTY. Milky Way?

JACK. The galaxy we live in, Betty.

BETTY. Oh. But, why did the Russians…

JACK. Soviets…

BETTY. …Soviets, set up missiles in Cuba in the first place?

JACK. To protect Cuba from the big, bad wolf, the United States of America.

BETTY. But, why? We aren't going to do anything bad to Cuba. *(silence)* Jack? Are we?

JACK. Well, Betty, you see, I did a bad thing…

BETTY. You did? What?

JACK. Oh, I tried to overthrow the Castro regime after I said I wouldn't. Damn! What made me think they could pull it off? Everybody knows Latins are lovers, not fighters. They'd rather be dancing the rumba or the mambo than to be fighting. In any case, this whole thing should come to a head, pardon the pun, *(He chuckles.)* …within the next couple of days and I hope we can come to some kind of peaceful resolution. I will try to keep you informed. Betty, you know what to do in case of a nuclear attack, don't you?

BETTY. Yes, Mr. President. Duck and cover.

JACK. Good girl! I have to go, Betty, Jackie is calling me…

BETTY. Oh, her…

JACK. Now, now, Betty, don't speak unkindly of the First Lady.

BETTY. I'm sorry. It's just that she gets all of the attention. It's all about Jackie and what she wore last night, what she's wearing today, what she'll be wearing tomorrow and people don't care about all the important things you're doing for the country.

(**JACK** *chuckles.*)

JACK. Oh, Betty, it comes with the territory. Besides, its better that way. It kind of keeps the heat off of me.

BETTY. Jack?

JACK. Yes, Betty?

BETTY. Do you really love Jackie? I mean, with all your heart and soul?

JACK. Of course, I do, Betty.

BETTY. And you don't cheat on her, do you? You don't go out with other women?

(silence)

JACK. Betty, I have to go…try to save the world.

BETTY. Oh, yes, of course.

JACK. You take care now.

BETTY. I will. Goodbye, Jack.

JACK. Goodbye, Betty.

(She hangs up.)

Scene Seven

(JOHNNY is in the living room when their father, CARLOS, now in his 40s enters carrying a paper bag. Before JOHNNY can say anything, CARLOS puts his finger to his lips and shushes him.)

CARLOS. Shhh… *(CARLOS looks around.)* Is Mom mad?

JOHNNY. Kinda…

CARLOS. What do you mean "kinda."

JOHNNY. Well, at first she was worried.

(CARLOS smiles at the thought.)

Then, she got annoyed. And then she got mad.

(CARLOS looks a little worried.)

But, I think she's getting over it.

(CARLOS grins.)

Where were you, Dad?

(CARLOS smiles.)

CARLOS. Taking care of business.

(JOHNNY smiles.)

A man's gotta do what a man's gotta do. You know what I mean? Look, there must be a girl you like..

JOHNNY. Lots of them…

CARLOS. Son, there are a lot of women in the world. Some are for marrying and having a family with and some are for…

(JOHNNY doesn't like what CARLOS is saying.)

Other things… You know what I mean?

JOHNNY. I think so…

ELENA. *(offstage)* Johnny!

(ELENA enters, sees CARLOS and stops.)

ELENA. When did you get back?

CARLOS. Just now.

(**BETTY** *enters.*)

BETTY. Daddy!

(She goes to hug him. **BOBBY** *enters, but doesn't speak. He gives* **CARLOS** *an accusatory look.)*

CARLOS. I have good news! You are looking at the new president of the *Porfirio Diaz* Club! I won by a landslide!

*(***ELENA*** isn't impressed.)*

I'll be introduced as the new president at the annual dance in a few weeks. I'll need a new suit and...

(He goes to **ELENA**.*)*

...you'll need a new dress because you're going to be the first lady of the club. I'll have to make a speech... *(He looks at the kids.)* You know what an honor this is? How important this is to me, to your mother, to all of us? Me, who came from nothing, to be the president of the Porfirio Diaz Club...

JOHNNY. Congratulations, Dad.

BETTY. But, Dad, didn't you hear the president?

JOHNNY. The Russians are going to attack us with nuclear missiles.

CARLOS. Not before the big dance.

BOBBY. How do you know, Dad?

CARLOS. I just do, that's all. *(He looks at them.)* What's the matter with you? Are you scared?

JOHNNY. I'm not, Bobby is.

*(***CARLOS*** shoots* **BOBBY** *a disapproving look.)*

CARLOS. What are you, a sissy?

BOBBY. No.

CARLOS. Where's Gina? I know Gina's not afraid. *(He calls out.)* Gina! ¡Ven paca! (Come here!)

(No response.)

BETTY. We already know what to do...

BOBBY. Duck and cover.

(**JOHNNY** *laughs.*)

JOHNNY. They've been practicing.

CARLOS. If you know what to do, why are you so worried?

BOBBY. Gina says it won't help anyway. She says we're all gonna burn to a crisp.

CARLOS. Oh, and what did you do, start crying?

(**JOHNNY** *snickers.*)

BOBBY. No.

CARLOS. You better not. I already told you about that.

ELENA. Leave him alone…

CARLOS. There you go, babying him again. (*to* **BOBBY**) What are you a mama's boy, huh?

BOBBY. No.

(**BOBBY** *sulks.* **CARLOS** *looks at the kids.*)

CARLOS. You really are scared, aren't you? Now, you listen to me. Nothing is going to happen to us. Do you think those missiles are aimed at Phoenix, Arizona? No. So, enough with the gloom and doom.

(*The kids look hopeful. They might survive after all.* **CARLOS** *tries to lighten things up.*)

Look what I got!

(*He takes 45 vinyls out of the bag one by one.*)

Something for the kids.

(*He hands a record to* **JOHNNY**.)

JOHNNY. Elvis!

(**BETTY** *grabs it.*)

BETTY. Love me tender!

(**CARLOS** *does an Elvis imitation and* **JOHNNY** *mimics him.*)

CARLOS. "Love me tender…"

JOHNNY. "…love me sweet."

(*He takes out another record.*)

CARLOS. And for you…

(He goes toward **ELENA** *and takes her in his arms.)*

Eydie Gorme and *Trio Los Panchos. (singing and dancing)* "Me importas tú, y tú, y tú…"

(The kids laugh at his antics.)

*(***ELENA** *pulls away and slaps* **CARLOS** *across the face, hard. She exits.)*

BETTY. Mom! Mom! What are you doing?

(The boys look confused. **BOBBY** *runs after* **ELENA**.*)*

BOBBY. Mom?

Scene Eight

(Music: "Shout"*)

(Lights up on **ELENA** *as she enters the bedroom.)*

*(***BOBBY** *sings the first line.*)*

*(***CARLOS** *enters and tries to caress her, but she pulls away from him.)*

*(***BOBBY** *sings ther second line.*)*

*(***ELENA** *shows* **CARLOS** *the shirt with the lipstick on it.)*

*(***BOBBY** *sings the third and fourth line.*)*

*(***CARLOS** *examines the shirt, smiles and shakes his head in denial.)*

*(***BOBBY** *sings the fifth line.*)*

(He brushes her hair back from her face and kisses it. **ELENA** *melts.)*

*(***BOBBY** *sings the seventh line.*)*

(She kisses him back. He pulls her to the bed.)

(Crossfade to: the kids cover their ears and sing and dance as **ELENA** *and* **CARLOS** *make love.)*

*(***BOBBY** *sings the eighth line.*)*

*(***BOBBY, JOHNNY, GINA,** *and* **BETTY** *sing the chorus of "Shout" together.*)*

(The music fades...)

---

*Please see Music Use Not on page 3

Scene Nine

(**ENRIQUE**'s wife, **MARI**, sits in the dark, listening to Agustin Lara on the record player, smoking a cigarette, drinking tequila. The song ends and the sound of the scratching needle continues. **ENRIQUE** enters.)

ENRIQUE. ¿Qué te pasa, Mari? (What's the matter, Mari?) Why are you sitting in the dark?

(No response. He removes the needle from the record. He goes to her.)

What's wrong, mi amor? (my love)

(She drinks.)

MARI. I don't know... I...

ENRIQUE. Have you been inside all day? I thought you were going shopping.

MARI. I can't... I... I don't know. No sé, Enrique. (I don't know, Enrique.)

(He sits next to her.)

I keep thinking about the baby...

ENRIQUE. Mari, don't. That was so long ago...

MARI. The baby, Enrique...would be fifteen...

ENRIQUE. Stop it! You can't stay in here all day crying about things you can't do anything about.

MARI. Let's go to San Francisco, Enrique. It's so pretty there. Or let's go live in México...

ENRIQUE. We can't, Mari. My job is here...

MARI. I hate it here! I always have. The heat, the dirt, the dust. Me sofoca. (It suffocates me.)

(An air raid siren sounds. She covers her ears.)

¡Ese pinche sonido, me tortura! ¡Abrázame, Enrique! Abrázame, abrázame... (That fuckin' sound tortures me! Hold me, Enrique! Hold me, hold me...)

(**ENRIQUE** holds **MARI** as the siren continues.)

Scene Ten

(BETTY, JOHNNY and BOBBY are in the living room watching television.)

BETTY. Don't worry. Jack… I mean, the president is going to protect us. He said he would and he will because he's a man of his word and he's Catholic.

JOHNNY. That's why *Nana* likes him because he's a Catholic.

BOBBY. What's so good about being Catholic?

JOHNNY. I don't know. But, *Nana* thinks its good.

BOBBY. *Nana* says they're going to kill the president because he's Catholic.

BETTY. Don't say that! Why would you say that?

BOBBY. I didn't say it. *Nana* did.

(GINA enters with a shoe in her hand.)

BETTY. *Nana* doesn't know anything.

JOHNNY. I'm gonna tell Mom you said that.

BETTY. What does she know? She's from Mexico.

BOBBY. So?

BETTY. So, she doesn't get it.

JOHNNY. Mom says it's because *Nana* grew up during the Mexican Revolution and there was a lot of violence and death and stuff like that.

BETTY. That's right. She thinks America is like Mexico. She doesn't know anything…

GINA. Have you ever tried talking to her?

BETTY. No. I don't speak Spanish…

GINA. So, don't say she doesn't know anything. You idiot.

BETTY. I'm gonna tell Dad you called me an idiot..

GINA. Go ahead and you'll see what you get!

(She threatens BETTY with her shoe.)

Idiot.

(pause)

GINA. *Nana* says that the name of Dad's club is the stupidest name she's ever heard because Porfirio Diaz was a dictator and he's the reason the Mexican Revolution happened in the first place.

JOHNNY. I'm gonna tell Dad what you said about the name of his club.

GINA. Go ahead. If he doesn't know his club is named after a military dictator, then he's an idiot...

(They gasp!)

...sss father.

(BETTY's confused..)

BETTY. What do you mean, if he doesn't know he's an idiot's father? That doesn't make any sense.

GINA. Yes, it does. But you don't understand because you're an idiot.

(BETTY flips GINA the finger.)

Mom!

ELENA. *(offstage)* What?

BETTY. Okay, okay, I'm sorry. Don't tell Mom.

GINA. Never mind... *(She threatens BETTY with her shoe.)* Do that again and you'll see what you get.

(BETTY exits.)

Has anybody seen my other shoe?

(The boys don't answer.)

I said has anybody seen my other shoe?!?

BOYS. No!

GINA. Well, don't just stand there! Look for it!

(They protest.)

Nobody leaves this house until you find my other shoe!

BOBBY. I'm gonna tell Mom.

GINA. I don't care.

JOHNNY. I'm gonna tell Dad.

GINA. If you do, I'll tell him you didn't feed the dog and if I get a beating, then so will you!

(JOHNNY *shuts up.*)

Now, go, look or I'll whip your ass!

BOBBY. You're mean!

GINA. And?

BOBBY. You just are.

(JOHNNY *enters with her shoe in his hand.*)

JOHNNY. Found it!

(GINA *grabs it and whacks him with it.*) Ouch!

GINA. Just in case you go snitching on me! *(calling out)* Betty, let's go! *(She threatens* BOBBY, *too.)* And you either!

(*She grabs her books and exits.*)

BOBBY. She's like "The Bad Seed."

JOHNNY. No, she's not. The Bad Seed pretended to be nice.

(BETTY *enters.*)

BETTY. Where's Gina?

BOBBY. She left.

BETTY. Without me? Damn it!

(BETTY *exits.* JOHNNY *and* BOBBY *look at each other.*)

JOHNNY. Mom calls it adolescence.

(*Air raid sirens sound.*)

TV VOICE. This is a test. This is only a test.

Scene Eleven

(**ELENA** *is ironing and* **ENRIQUE** *sits at the table.*)

ENRIQUE. So, he's back?

ELENA. Yes, with a bag full of gifts.

ENRIQUE. And full of guilt, I bet, *el cabrón. (the ass)*

ELENA. Full of explanations. Let's put it that way.

ENRIQUE. Do you believe him?

ELENA. I don't know. *¿Pero que voy a ser, Kiki? (But what can I do, Kiki?)* I told him I'm getting a job.

ENRIQUE. *¿Deberas? (Really?)* And what did he say?

ELENA. He laughed. I don't think he believes me.

ENRIQUE. *¿Y los bukis? (And the kids?)* Who will take care of the kids?

ELENA. They're old enough to take care of themselves. *¿Qué piensas? (What do you think?)*

ENRIQUE. It's up to you, but if you were my wife...

(*He shakes his head.*)

ELENA. Sometimes... I think it's as much my fault as it is his. I mean, maybe he needs a different kind of woman. You know, the kind who can laugh and be sexy and drink and smoke cigarettes and...

ENRIQUE. *Es un pinche buey, Elena. (He's a fuckin' ass, Elena.)*

ELENA. I'm boring, I'm a prude, "a goody two shoes," he always says...

ENRIQUE. Hey, hey, hey... Don't do this to yourself. Carlos doesn't know how lucky he is.

(*a brief look*)

ELENA. *¿Y Mari? ¿Cómo está? (And Mari? How is she?)*

ENRIQUE. *Igual. (The same.)* She just stays inside all day long. Says she wants to move to *San Francisco* or go back to *México*.

ELENA. Back? *¿De veras? ¿Qué vas a ser? (Really? What are you gonna do?)*

(He shrugs.)

ENRIQUE. *No sé. (Don't know.)* I can't move to *México.* And do what? I'm from here, born and raised. In *México* I feel like a gringo and here I feel like a Mexican. *Que pinche suerte. (What luck.)* I can't speak good English and I can't speak good Spanish… *Estoy jodido. (I'm screwed.)*

(They laugh. Then, silence.)

I don't know… She just cries all the time. We're going to see the doctor…

(CARLOS enters with a six pack of Coors.)

CARLOS. Who's going to the doctor?

(ENRIQUE and ELENA are a little startled.)

ENRIQUE. *Mari,* she's not feeling well.

CARLOS. Is she still…?

(He does a "crazy" motion to his head.)

ELENA. Carlos!

(CARLOS pats ENRIQUE on the back.)

CARLOS. Oh, you know what I mean… *(CARLOS gets up close behind ELENA.)* What's for dinner, Elena? I'm starved.

(She pulls away from, embarrassed.)

ELENA. I'll get it started.

(As she exits, he pats her on the butt.)

ENRIQUE. So, you took a trip, I hear.

(CARLOS takes out two beers and hands one to ENRIQUE.)

CARLOS. What did she say? Was she mad? I came back and she was angry because she found lipstick on my collar. *(He smiles.)* I told her… I don't remember what I told her…but she believed me.

(**CARLOS** *lights a cigarette.*)

CARLOS. I drove down to *Nogales* with Pancho and we met some… (*He outlines curves with his arms.*)

…*buenotas. Con unas…* (*…good ones. With some…*)

(*He describes big boobs with his hands.*) Next time we go down there, I'll let you know.

ENRIQUE. No, thanks. I don't like *Nogales*.

CARLOS. No?

ENRIQUE. I don't know. The poor people begging, the kids selling things in the street. I just don't like it.

CARLOS. *Compadre, (Buddy,)* you've always been the sensitive type. *Pero, eres casi joto, hombre. (But, you're like a homosexual, man.)*

(**CARLOS** *laughs.* **ENRIQUE** *is not amused.*)

¡Pero te quiero, buey! (But, I love you, asshole.)

(**CARLOS** *gets serious.*)

I love my wife, Enrique.

ENRIQUE. *¿De veras? (Really?)*

CARLOS. *Seguro que sí. (Of course I do.)* I married her, didn't I?

ENRIQUE. *Pues entonces trátala bien, cabrón. (Then treat her well, asshole.)*

(**CARLOS** *looks at* **ENRIQUE.** *He takes a drag.*)

CARLOS. To be faithful, Kiki… Some men can, some can't. Maybe you can… (*pause*) But, I can't… (*silence*) We got married during the war. I was eighteen and she was fifteen. Everyone was getting married then, remember?

ENRIQUE. Yup. Getting married without even knowing if we'd make it back alive.

(*They sit on the thought for a sec.*)

CARLOS. I couldn't go to the war because I hurt my leg working in the mine. I wanted to go so bad. My good friend, Freddy, he died in the war. Did you know that?

ENRIQUE. Yeah, you told me.

CARLOS. I did?

ENRIQUE. Yeah, when we were *pedos (drunk)* one time.

CARLOS. He was like a big brother to me. When my mom died, he took me under his wing, talked to me about life... things my dad never talked about. The funny thing is he didn't want to go to war and I did. I couldn't, but he did, and he died. Then, I asked Elena to marry me. I guess I wanted to make sure that I had what Freddie always wanted but never had, a life – a wife and kids, a home.

ENRIQUE. *Pues, sí. (Well, yes.)*

CARLOS. We lost a lot of boys in that war, didn't we?

ENRIQUE. We sure did.

(They sit on that thought for a sec.)

And those of us who did make it back, well... I remember coming home on the bus, looking sharp in my uniform feeling all American *y la chingada. (and shit)* Pull into a depot in Texas, try to get a bite to eat and there's a sign that says, "No negroes and no Mexicans allowed." I remember feeling something that day. Something ugly. *(pause)* I try not to think about it too much *porque si me pongo a pensar... (because if I think about it)*

(CARLOS looks at ENRIQUE and smiles.)

CARLOS. Don't get so serious on me, *cabrón. (asshole)* You're gonna make me cry.

(They laugh.)

I know you think I'm a *cabrón...* and I am. But, I love my family and I love my wife.

(Musical Interlude: 'Piel Canela')*

---

*Please see Music Use Not on page 3

Scene Twelve

(ELENA, GINA *and* BETTY *are setting the table for dinner.*)

ELENA. *(calling out)* Boys, Carlos, come and eat.

(CARLOS *enters with a newspaper in his hand.*)

CARLOS. Look here's an article about the elections. *(reads:)* "Carlos Garcia was elected president of the Mexican-American civic club, *El Club Porfirio Diaz.*"

BETTY. Really, daddy? Let me see.

(CARLOS *hands* BETTY *the paper.*)

(She reads:) "The installation dinner and dance will take place on Saturday, October 27, 1962 at 7:00 pm."

GINA. If we're still alive by then.

CARLOS. *(to* ELENA*)* Did you buy a new dress?

ELENA. Yes…

(JOHNNY *and* BOBBY *enter and sit at the table, ready to be served.*)

(to the boys) Did you wash your hands? ¿A ver? *(Let's see?)*

(*The boys show* ELENA *their clean hands.* BETTY, *still looking at the newspaper:*)

BETTY. Oh, look, President Kennedy…

ELENA. Betty, get the beans.

(CARLOS *takes the paper back and continues to read. The dog barks.* ELENA *looks at the boys.*)

Did you feed the dog?

(The boys look at each other.)

(to CARLOS*)* …They never feed the dog. The dog is starving to death. Every day I ask them "Did

you feed the dog?" and it's always somebody else's turn.

CARLOS. Bobby, go feed the dog.

BOBBY. Why do I have to? Why can't Johnny…

CARLOS. Because I said so.

BOBBY. But…

CARLOS. Now!

> (**BOBBY** *sulks off as the women put food on the table.*)

ELENA. I ask them to clean the yard. Have you seen the yard? It's embarrassing. And have you seen the grass? It's brown, not green.

> (**CARLOS** *looks at* **JOHNNY**.)

CARLOS. Did you hear your mother? You boys better clean that yard and water the grass.

JOHNNY. Yes, sir.

ELENA. Have you seen their rooms? I have to be after them to clean them. They leave a mess in the kitchen and the backyard is full of junk. I get tired of having to tell them. I guess they want to live in a pigsty.

> (**BOBBY** *enters.*)

BOBBY. Okay, Mom! Is that all you can do, nag?

CARLOS. Don't talk to your mother like that!

BOBBY. Why not? You do!

CARLOS. What? What did you say to me?

BOBBY. Nothing!

> (**CARLOS** *gets up and removes his belt.* **BOBBY** *begins to cry, runs out and* **CARLOS** *goes after him.*)

CARLOS. You wanna cry? You wanna cry?

JOHNNY. No, Dad, don't hit him.

BETTY. No, Daddy!

ELENA. Carlos!

> (*We hear* **CARLOS** *beating* **BOBBY** *with the belt, hard.* **GINA** *looks at* **ELENA**.)

GINA. Are you happy now?

 (JOHNNY, BETTY, GINA. *sing the end of "Shout."**)

 (*The song gets louder and* BETTY *covers her ears.*)

---

* Please see Music Use Note on Page 3

Scene Thirteen

(The phone rings. **BETTY** *runs to answer it.)*

BETTY. Hello?

FIDEL CASTRO. *(Spanish accent)* Betty, *soy yo, (it's me,)* Fidel Castro.

BETTY. It's about time you returned my call!

FIDEL CASTRO. I am very busy, Betty, trying to protect my people, trying to save my island.

BETTY. Well, you're going about it the wrong way.

FIDEL CASTRO. Oh, Betty, I can already tell, you've been brain washed by the Yankee Imperialists.

BETTY. Why? Why did you have to chummy up with the Russians…

FIDEL CASTRO. Soviets…

BETTY. You know who I mean.

FIDEL CASTRO. I had no choice, Betty. What choice did I have? My people have to eat.

BETTY. So, you're going to destroy the whole world?

FIDEL CASTRO. Betty, the missiles are there for protection only. We are a tiny, little island, Betty, ninety miles away from the largest super power in the world.

BETTY. Okay, what if Jack… I mean, President Kennedy promises not to attack Cuba. Would that work?

FIDEL CASTRO. How can I believe him, Betty? He promised before. He is like a cheating husband who can't be trusted.

BETTY. What if he swears on his mother…

FIDEL CASTRO. No…

BETTY. …or on the Catholic Bible.

(silence)

FIDEL CASTRO. The Catholic Bible? You know, Betty, I went to Jesuit school my whole life…

BETTY. So, would that make you tell the Russ…the Soviets to take down the missiles?

FIDEL CASTRO. Well... I think that would be a possible compromise...

BETTY. Let me talk to the president and see what he says, okay?

FIDEL CASTRO. Okay, Betty and I will discuss with Nakita.

BETTY. Okay, bye Fidel.

FIDEL CASTRO. Bye, Betty. *Patria o muerte. Vencéremos. (Land or death. We shall overcome.)*

BETTY. What?

FIDEL CASTRO. Never mind.

> (**BETTY** *smiles and hangs up the phone. She picks up a photo of JFK and sings the first and second verses of "Piel Canela."*)*

Scene Fourteen

(CARLOS and ELENA are in the bedroom. They are dressed to the "T's" for the dance. He is wearing a nice suit and tie, she is wearing a black spaghetti strap cocktail dress, pearls and pumps. She sits in front of the vanity, putting on the finishing touches.)

CARLOS. You look sexy.

ELENA. I do?

(He comes close.)

CARLOS. Uh huh. I like the dress.

ELENA. Maybe a little too low in the front?

CARLOS. Uh uh.

(He tries to touch her breasts.)

ELENA. Carlos…

(She puts on her lipstick. He smiles.)

CARLOS. When I was a boy I would watch my mom get ready to go out. She'd walk around in her slip with pin curls in her hair. I'd start getting butterflies in my stomach because I knew she was going out and I was always afraid that she wouldn't come back. That something would happen to her. That I'd lose her. That she'd never come back. Meet a man and run away with him. I'd watch her get ready to go out, wanting to cry. She'd put on her red lipstick, take the pins out and her long black hair would fall on her shoulders. She'd slip on her dress and her high heels, dab some perfume behind her ears, on her neck and down between her breasts. She'd give me a kiss, grab her bag and walk out the door, her high heels clicking as I'd watch her disappear into the night, sick to my stomach, tears rolling and I'd sit there and wait and wait and wait. I'd usually fall asleep waiting and wake up when she was putting me to bed smelling of whiskey, cigarettes and perfume and I loved that smell because it meant she was home. I loved that smell. Still do...

(He sits on the memory for a sec.)

Are you excited about tonight?

ELENA. A little nervous.

CARLOS. Nervous? I'm the one who has to give a speech. Then, I'll introduce you as the new first lady...

ELENA. That's what I'm nervous about, I think.

(He smiles.)

CARLOS. Have a couple of drinks. Loosen up a little...

ELENA. Okay.

CARLOS. You seem so wound-up all the time.

ELENA. You would be too with four kids and a husband who... *(She stops herself.)*

(CARLOS smiles.)

CARLOS. Look, let's try to have a good time. I'm the president and you're the first lady. Let's celebrate. *(He looks at her.)* Elena...

ELENA. Okay.

(Musical Interlude: "Piel Canela" by Félix Manuel Rodríguez Capó.)*

*(ELENA sings four lines.**)*

---

*Please see Music Use Note on page 3
**Please see Music Use Note on page 3

Scene Fifteen

(The band plays as **ENRIQUE** *enters and finds* **ELENA** *is sitting alone at the dance. She's had a few drinks and is a little tipsy.)*

ENRIQUE. *¿Qué haces aquí solita? (Why are you here all alone?)*

ELENA. Not too much. Where's Mari?

ENRIQUE. She didn't want to come. *¿Y el cabrón, dónde está? (Where's the ass?)*

ELENA. Oh, he's dancing with everybody except me. I guess he has to. He's the new president.

*(*ELENA *sings three lines from "Rico Vacilon" by Rosendo Ruiz Quevedo.*)*

(Song continues underneath.)

ENRIQUE. Come on. You look too pretty to be a wallflower.

*(*ENRIQUE *sings the same three lines from "Rico Vacilon."*)*

*(*ELENA *gets up to dance with* ENRIQUE. *She's woozy and he has to help her stay steady.)*

ENRIQUE. *¡Aguas! (Careful!)* Hold on to me.

(song ends)

VOICE. *(offstage) ¡Y ahora les presento el nuevo presidente del Club Porfirio Diaz, Carlos Garcia! (And now I present you the new president of the Porfirio Diaz Club, Carlos Garcia!)*

(Applause. CARLOS *goes to the microphone.)*

CARLOS. *¡Muchas gracias! Es un honor.* It's an honor to be here tonight as your new president.

(Applause. He clears his throat.)

Thank you. When I joined this club a few years ago, I joined because I wanted to get involved in our community, the Mexican-American community. I am

---

*Please see Music Use Note on page 3

proud to be an American and I know that we live in the greatest country in the world. Many of us have fought for our country, died for our country. But, we are also proud of our Mexican heritage and we like our Mexican music and our Mexican food and when we get together we are reminded of the fact that no matter where we are in the world, we are and always will be Mexicans... *Mexicanos de corazon. (Mexicans at heart.)*

(applause)

My mother, God rest her soul, waved the Mexican flag and the American flag, as we do here today. I will do my best to be a good president and I thank you for giving me the opportunity to serve *¡y que viva México! (and long live México!)*

CROWD. *¡Qué viva!*

CARLOS. And now, I'd like to introduce my wife, the first lady of *El Club Civico Porfirio Diaz*... Elena Garcia.

(**ELENA**, *a little wobbly, puts on a fake smile and waves at the crowd. Applause.*)

I hope you are all enjoying yourselves!

ELENA. I'm enjoying myself!

CARLOS. Now, let's all have a good time. *Gracias.*

(**CARLOS** *sings four lines from "Corazón De Melon" by Los Hermanos Rigual.*[*])

(**ELENA** *drags* **ENRIQUE** *onto the dance floor. She holds on to him tight.*)

ELENA. *(to herself)* One, two, cha-cha-cha, One, two, cha-cha-cha. And turn!

(She tries to do a cha cha turn. She slips and falls.)

(Music stops. Everything and everybody stops and looks. **ELENA** *is in the middle of the dance floor on her ass. She looks around...)*

---

*Please see Music Use Note on page 3

ELENA. *(cont.)* Oops.

> *(She starts to laugh.* **ENRIQUE** *picks her up as* **CARLOS** *approaches.)*

CARLOS. ¿*Qué chingados estás haciendo?* *(What the fuck are you doing?)*

> *(They move off of the dance floor.)*

You're drunk.

ELENA. You told me to have a good time.

> *(***CARLOS** *slaps* **ELENA** *and* **ENRIQUE** *steps in.)*

ENRIQUE. Carlos! ¿*Qué te pasa buey?* *(What's wrong with you, ass?)*

> *(He looks around.)*

You're making a scene *cabrón (asshole).*

> *(***CARLOS** *catches himself, looks around.* **ENRIQUE** *helps* **ELENA** *catch her bearings.)*

So, she had a little too much to drink. *Cálmate. (Calm down.)*

> *(They stare at each other for a second.)*

Look, I'll drive her home. You stay here. You can't leave.

ELENA. Yeah, you can't leave. You're the new president!

> *(***CARLOS** *thinks on it.)*

CARLOS. *Ándale pues… (Alright then…)* *(to* **ENRIQUE***)* Get her out of here. She's drunk.

> *(as* **ENRIQUE** *leads* **ELENA** *out –)*

ELENA. I've been kicked out of better places. *(She laughs.)* Well, not really, but… ¡*Viva México!* *(Long live México!)*

> *(***ENRIQUE** *takes* **ELENA** *and leaves.)*

Scene Sixteen

(Musical Interlude: "Love Hurts"*)

*(**GINA** and **RUDY** are sitting underneath the weeping willow tree. It is quiet, except for the chirping of the crickets. **RUDY** slowly moves to hold **GINA**'s hand. She doesn't even notice because her mind is somewhere else. They sit in silence for a while.)*

GINA. The locusts are coming

RUDY. They are?

GINA. Uh huh. I read in the paper that people saw this thing in the sky and they thought it was a nuclear cloud, but it turned out to be a swarm of locusts, a plague.

RUDY. Like in the bible?

GINA. Uh huh... A plague of locusts devouring everything in its tracks and it's headed our way. It's crazy. All these grasshoppers come together in a swarm that migrates and a swarm can be hundreds of miles long and can travel hundreds of miles in one day and they can eat entire crops, leaving nothing behind but stems and bare branches.

RUDY. What makes them do that? What do they want?

(She shrugs.)

GINA. To survive, I guess.

RUDY. A hungry swarm eating everything in sight. Sounds like my family.

(They laugh.)

I told my mom about us.

GINA. What? What about us?

RUDY. That you're my girlfriend...for now. She's really happy. She likes you.

GINA. She hardly knows me.

---

* Please see Music Use Note on page 3

RUDY. But, she likes you. She said she likes you.

GINA. Didn't you tell her that I'm mean and that I'm mad all the time?

RUDY. No, you're not. You're not mean, you're just honest.

GINA. I wish I could tell people what they want to hear, but I can't. It's a curse the women in our family have.

(**RUDY** *laughs.*)

RUDY. A curse?

GINA. Don't laugh, it's true.

(**RUDY** *stops laughing.*)

Somebody, one of our ancestors, made a promise along time ago. I think it was supposed to be a good thing, but, my *Nana* calls it a curse. The women in our family can't lie.

RUDY. Do you believe in that stuff?

GINA. Yeah…because no matter how hard I try, I can't keep my big mouth shut.

RUDY. So, that explains it. It's a curse. There's nothing you can do about it.

GINA. Can I tell you something and you promise not to tell?

RUDY. Promise.

GINA. Sometimes… I know it's wrong, but sometimes, I look at my mom and the way she is around my dad and I hate her. I hate her for not standing up to him and I hate her for not telling him how she feels. I hate her for letting him beat us and I hate her for snitching on us because she knows he will. Sometimes, I just feel like hurting someone and I hit my brothers with my shoe and I pull my sister's hair. I don't know why. I can't help it.

(*He puts his arm around her.*)

RUDY. I'm the luckiest guy in the world.

(*She looks up at the tree.*)

GINA. I sure hope the locusts don't eat my tree.

RUDY. Our tree. I'm gonna miss you Gina.

(He tries to get romantic. He kisses her gently. **GINA** *likes it, but tries to skip the subject.)*

GINA. Do you know where weeping willows come from?

(He kisses her again and it gets hot and heavy.)

RUDY. Can we go to the car?

GINA. No, I already told you…

*(***RUDY*** *tries to touch her breasts.)*

Stop it, Rudy.

RUDY. Please. Gina, it's my last night.

(They kiss some more.)

(The sound and lights of a car make them stop.)

GINA. Shh…

(They see **ELENA** *and* **ENRIQUE** *walk toward the house.)*

Scene Seventeen

(ENRIQUE helps ELENA into the house and into her bedroom. He sits her on the bed and she flops backward.)

ENRIQUE. Whoa. *Cuidado…* *(Careful…)*

ELENA. Can I ask you a question, Kiki? A serious one?

(He pulls off her shoes.)

ENRIQUE. *¿A ver? ¿Qué? (Let's see? What?)*

ELENA. Am I as drunk as I think I am?

ENRIQUE. Drunker, probably.

ELENA. He said to celebrate.

(ENRIQUE covers ELENA with a blanket and as he's going to leave. She grabs his hand.)

Kiki?

ENRIQUE. *¿Qué pasó? (What?)*

ELENA. Am I pretty?

ENRIQUE. You're beautiful.

ELENA. Kiki?

ENRIQUE. Huh?

ELENA. Will you kiss me?

(He looks at her.)

Please…

(ENRIQUE kisses ELENA and she kisses him back long and passionately. GINA enters and sees them, but they don't see her. GINA exits.)

(ENRIQUE pulls away from ELENA.)

ENRIQUE. I better go. *(ENRIQUE leaves.)*

(GINA runs back to RUDY and kisses him.)

GINA. Come on… *(She takes him by the hand.)*

RUDY. Where we going?

GINA. To your car.

(They exit.)

(**ENRIQUE** *comes out of the house:*)

(**ENRIQUE** *sings the fifth verse of "Love Hurts."*")

(**ENRIQUE** *exits.*)

(**GINA** *and* **RUDY** *enter.*)

(**RUDY** *sings the first two lines of the fourth verse.**)

(**GINA** *sings the last two lines of the fourth verse.**)

(**RUDY** *and* **GINA** *sings the first five lines of the fifth verse.**)

(**ALL** *sing the last line.**)

(**GINA** *and* **RUDY** *kiss. He exits. She sits below the weeping willow tree. The sound of the locusts grows.*)

(*Footage: the end of the Cuban Missile crisis*)

End of Act One

ACT TWO

Scene One

(Music: "Mr. Postman"*)

(Lights up. The locusts have devoured the weeping willow tree. All that is left are bare branches. The kids are dancing the Mash Potato in the living room. **BETTY** *is looking through the mail.)*

*(***GINA*** sings the first eleven lines of "Mr. Postman."*)*

*(***BETTY*** is on the phone. JFK's silhouette appears.)*

JACK. That was a close call, wasn't it, Betty?

BETTY. No kidding!

JACK. Thanks for all your help.

BETTY. Oh, please. Don't mention it. Did you do what I told you to do?

JACK. What? Oh, yes, yes… I promised not to invade Cuba and…

BETTY. …you better keep your promise this time.

JACK. I will, Betty, I swear.

BETTY. On what?

JACK. On the Catholic Bible.

BETTY. Okay, good!

JACK. Betty, don't tell anyone, but…

BETTY. Yes?

JACK. Promise?

---

*Please see Music Use Note on page 3

BETTY. I promise.

JACK. On what?

BETTY. On my mother's grave.

> *(pause.)*

JACK. *(whispers)* I was scared, Betty. Really scared. I didn't know what those damned Russians...

BETTY. ...Soviets...

JACK. ...Soviets were going to do. *(He laughs loud, then composes himself.)* Well, Betty, gotta go.

BETTY. Wait. Jack, please say it. Please, just once.

JACK. Betty...

BETTY. Just once, please...

JACK. *(whispers)* Ask not what your country can do for you. Ask what you can do for your country.

> **(BETTY** *sighs.)*

Goodbye, Betty.

BETTY. Goodbye, Jack.

> *(She hangs up.)*

Scene Two

(**GINA** *enters.*)

GINA. Did the mail come?

(**BETTY** *doesn't answer.*)

I said, did the mail come?

BETTY. Yes, but nothing for you. Just bills. We got a notice from the light company. They're gonna shut it off if Mom doesn't pay.

GINA. You love Dad so much. Why don't you call him and tell him to pay? Or is he too busy with his new girlfriend?

BETTY. He doesn't have a girlfriend. I asked him and he said the only reason he moved out is because Mom started working. He's sad. He thinks she doesn't love him anymore. He didn't want her to work and she went and got a job.

GINA. You have got to be the stupidest girl in the world. Do you believe him? You're worse than Mom!

(**GINA** *looks through the mail.*)

BETTY. Looking for a letter from Rudy? I thought you didn't like him.

GINA. Shut up.

BETTY. Why are you so mean?

GINA. I don't know, I just am. I was born that way. I'm the devil, okay.

BETTY. That's why Rudy hasn't written to you, because you're mean! You were mean to him…

GINA. Shut up. He can't write yet. He can't write until he's done with boot camp.

BETTY. That's not true. Nancy's brother is in boot camp and he writes.

GINA. Liar.

BETTY. I'm not lying.

(**GINA** *begins to exit. But, before she does, she pulls on* **BETTY**'s *hair.*)

BETTY. Ow, I'm gonna tell Dad..

GINA. Dad's not here anymore you little kiss ass!

BETTY. I'm gonna tell Mom you said kiss ass!

GINA. Go ahead! You just said it too!

(**BETTY** *looks confused. As* **GINA** *exits* **BETTY** *flips her off behind her back.* **GINA** *turns around and catches her.*)

You little bitch!

(**GINA** *raises one leg and puts her two fists on both sides. A bigger flip off!* **BETTY**'s *mouth drops open.* **GINA** *exits, triumphant.*)

(*Footage: JFK's Civil Rights Address, June 11, 1963*)

JFK'S VOICE. Good evening, my fellow citizens:

This afternoon, following a series of threats and defiant statements, the presence of Alabama National Guardsmen was required on the University of Alabama to carry out the final and unequivocal order of the United States District Court of the Northern District of Alabama. That order called for the admission of two clearly qualified young Alabama residents who happened to have been born Negro. That they were admitted peacefully on the campus is due in good measure to the conduct of the students of the University of Alabama, who met their responsibilities in a constructive way. I hope that every American, regardless of where he lives, will stop and examine his conscience about this and other related incidents. This Nation was founded by men of many nations and backgrounds. It was founded on the principle that all men are created equal, and that the rights of every man are diminished when the rights of one man are threatened.

Scene Three

(ELENA, BOBBY and JOHNNY lie on a blanket and pillows on the grass outside. BOBBY has his head on ELENA's lap. She strokes his hair. She's trying to keep it together.)

BOBBY. I like sleeping out here, Mom. I like looking up at the sky.

JOHNNY. Look, a shooting star!

BOBBY. Where?

JOHNNY. You missed it.

(BETTY and GINA enter with their own blanket.)

BETTY. Are we really gonna sleep outside, Mom?

ELENA. Yes, it's cooler out here.

BETTY. What if somebody sees us?

GINA. Who cares. If you wanna sleep inside with no cooler, go ahead.

(BETTY slaps a mosquito on her arm.)

BETTY. These mosquitos are eating me alive.
How can we live without electricity?

GINA. We don't have a choice, do we?

JOHNNY. When are we gonna pay the light bill, Mom?

ELENA. Friday. As soon as I get paid.

BETTY. Friday? Two more days?

GINA. *(mocking BETTY)* "Two more days," Shut up!

ELENA. Stop, Gina. It won't be so hot tomorrow.

JOHNNY. Yeah, only ninety.

GINA. People lived without electricity for centuries. It's only been in homes for around forty years or so.

BETTY. Thanks for the lecture, Einstein.

(GINA gives her the big flip off. BETTY throws one back. The boys giggle. ELENA doesn't even notice.)

When's Daddy coming back home, Mom?

(GINA *smacks* BETTY.)

BETTY. *(cont.)* Ouch!

ELENA. Gina!

GINA. It was a mosquito!

(GINA *gives* BETTY *a "Don't-ask-Mom-about-Dad" look.*
BETTY *looks up at the stars.*)

BETTY. Look at all the stars… I guess it's not so bad out
here, Mom.

GINA. We can look for the constellations.

BETTY. No, thanks. *(silence)* When I get married…

BOBBY. If you get married…

JOHNNY. If you can find someone desperate enough.

GINA. Or stupid enough.

ELENA. Quiet. Go on, *m'ija (my daughter)* …

BETTY. I want a beautiful wedding, with a beautiful gown
and a handsome groom with blonde hair…

JOHNNY. A paddy boy?

BETTY. What's wrong with paddy boys?

ELENA. Nothing.

GINA. Yeah, I guess they're better than Mexican boys.

BOBBY. Hey!

JOHNNY. Maybe you'll marry a colored boy.

BETTY. Maybe I will, so what?

GINA. Then Mom's family wouldn't talk to you because her
family doesn't like colored people.

ELENA. What? Your cousin Alice married a colored boy…

GINA. And your family disowned her. They still don't talk
to her.

JOHNNY. Really, Mom?

GINA. It's true, Mom, isn't it?

ELENA. Yes, it's true.

BETTY. Didn't they hear what the president said about
when one man's rights are diminished? Geez!

JOHNNY. That won't ever happen to us.

GINA. Why because you only like paddy girls like Arna Jean and Betty Lou?

JOHNNY. No, because nobody's going to fall in love with either one of you, no matter what color they are.

BETTY. That's so funny, I forgot to laugh. *(silence)* When I get married, I'm never gonna work. I'm gonna stay home and take care of my kids that way my husband... *(She catches herself.)* ...will be happy.

GINA. I'm never getting married.

ELENA. Gina, why?

(GINA shrugs.)

GINA. I don't want to. I wanna go to college, do something with my life.

ELENA. But, you want a family, don't you?

GINA. Uh uh, once you have kids, it's over. I mean, look at you.

BETTY. Gina!

GINA. I'm being honest. It's a curse remember. Just 'cause Mom never tells the truth...

BOBBY. Don't be mean to Mom, Gina. Shut up!

ELENA. It's okay. She's right. It's true. Once you have kids, there's no going back. Once you have 'em, you're stuck with them and you have to figure out how to take care of them whether you like it or not.

(The kids are surprised by ELENA's candor.)

BETTY. Gee, Mom, don't try to hide your feelings or anything. Is that how you feel about us?

BOBBY. That makes me sad, Mom.

(ELENA hugs BOBBY.)

ELENA. You see, Gina. Telling the truth has consequences. You haven't learned that yet. But, you will, some day. *(ELENA looks at her kids.)* And, no, I'm not sorry I have you kids. Yes, I was young when I had you, but I'm glad I did. I mean, look at you.

GINA. Yeah, look at us.

(They look at each other and laugh. ELENA has to laugh too.)

(Silence. Crickets, mosquitos, stars...)

BOBBY. Look, a shooting star!

(They all look up.)

JOHNNY. Cool.

ELENA. Next one we see, let's all make a wish, want to?

(They all look up.)

BOBBY. There's one!

ELENA. Okay, make a wish. You first, Bobby.

BOBBY. I wish that I make a lot of money so that I can buy Mom lots of pretty clothes so she'll look those ladies in Vogue Magazine.. And I'll buy her a summer house in Los Angeles, where it's not so hot and where Mom can be close to her family and *Nana Esperanza.*

(JOHNNY laughs at BOBBY.)

JOHNNY. Vogue Magazine? What a candyass.

ELENA. Shh. Go on, Johnny...

JOHNNY. Well, let's see. I'm already handsome... I guess... I wish that I become a famous musician and that I make lots of money so that I can buy Mom a house and clothes and that I have lots of girlfriends. But, of course, that's a given.

GINA. Oh, brother.

BETTY. My turn. I wish that one day I'll meet President Kennedy and that I can tell him how proud I am of him and everything he's done for our country and... let's see. Oh...and that I find a beautiful rainbow with a pot of gold at the end of it...

(The kids groan.)

...so that we can buy food and pay for the light bill.

ELENA. Go on, Gina...

GINA. I don't wish anything.

ELENA. Come on, Gina. You have to wish something.

BETTY. I know what she wishes. She wishes she would get a letter from Rudy.

GINA. Shut up!

ELENA. I wish you would stop saying shut up!

BOBBY. Mom, was that your wish?

ELENA. No!

GINA. Okay, I do have a wish.

(They all wait.)

I wish we had a different life.

BETTY. I wish Mom and Dad loved each other more than anything else in the world…

JOHNNY. I wish Dad would come home and stay home.

BOBBY. I wish Dad was like the father on "Leave it to Beaver" and he would say stuff like *(imitates Ward Cleaver)* "Son, I'm proud of you…"
What's your wish, Mom?

ELENA. It's a secret.

(silence)

(Music: "Mr. Sandman"*)

*(**BOBBY, JOHNNY, BETTY,** and **GINA** alternate singing seven lines.*)*

---

*Please see Music Use Note on page 3

Scene Four

(**ELENA** *is in the house dialing the phone.*)

MARI. *(offstage) ¿Bueno? ¿Bueno? ("Hello? Hello?")*

    (**ELENA** *hangs up.*)

Scene Five

(Lights up on **RUDY** *in a uniform. He's reading a letter to* **GINA**.*)*

RUDY. Dear Gina, I don't know if you want me to write to you or not. But, here it goes. I know what the deal was. Two weeks. But, they were the best two weeks of my life and I can't stop thinking about you and your frown and the way you smell and how good it felt to make love to you…

GINA. Dear Rudy, Please don't fall in love with me. I am not the kind of girl you deserve. You should find a girl who is good and kind and deserves to be loved by you. That girl is not me. You are the sweetest boy in the world. Please forget about me. Gina. P.S. I'm expecting a baby and I need money to try to get rid of it. Can you send me some money as soon as possible…

RUDY. Dear Gina, I want to marry you. I want you to have the baby…

GINA. Dear Rudy, I don't want the baby. I don't want to get married. It always turns out bad. Please, send me the money before it's too late.

RUDY. Dear Gina, I won't send you money…

GINA. Dear Rudy, I don't need your crappy money!

Scene Six

(The kids are in the living room.)

JOHNNY. I'm starved.

BOBBY. Mom said she's gonna bring us some potato pancakes. The restaurant owner is going to give her the left over ones.

BETTY. I'm sick of those damned potato pancakes.

JOHNNY. Good, more for me.

GINA. Shut your trap.

JOHNNY. I'm gonna tell Mom you said…

GINA. I'm gonna tell Mom you're hungry.

JOHNNY. No, don't tell her. I'm not hungry.

BETTY. Then why did you say you were? Why is everybody afraid to tell Mom that we're hungry? We're starving to death, she has to know.

GINA. Because there's nothing she can do about it, Betty. She's working two jobs and she doesn't make enough to feed your big fat mouth. So, what's the point?

BETTY. If Dad doesn't come back, we're gonna lose the house. I heard Mom talking to *Nana* on the phone and she was asking her for money for the house payment. She said, if we don't pay the payment we're gonna lose the house.

GINA. Be quiet, Betty.

(BETTY begins to cry.)

BETTY. I'm hungry, Gina…

GINA. Betty, stop it. We can't just sit here and wait for those god-damned potato pancakes. How much money do you have?

JOHNNY. None.

GINA. What about your paper route money?

JOHNNY. I gave it to Mom for the bus.

(GINA goes through BETTY's purse.)

BETTY. Gina, what are you doing?

(**GINA** *pulls out 50 cents.*)

That's my baby sitting money!

GINA. And?

BETTY. I'm saving up for my prom dress!

GINA. Has anybody asked you to the prom?

BETTY. No…

GINA. Then, you ain't going!

BETTY. Just cuz you don't save your money…

GINA. I give all my money to Mom! That's why I got a job, to help Mom you stupid ass! Now let's go get some food.

BETTY. With 50 cents?

JOHNNY. You can buy bread…

BOBBY. And bologna!

GINA. We'll buy what we can and the rest we'll… (*She stops.*)

(*The kids look at her.*)

Go get Mom's coat and I'll get mine.

BETTY. Gina…

GINA. Go get it.

JOHNNY. Gina, are you gonna steal food?

GINA. If you tell Mom, I'm not gonna give you any. Are you gonna tell her?

(*pause*)

JOHNNY. No.

(*They look at* **BOBBY**. *He is scared, but he answers –*)

BOBBY. No.

(**BETTY** *enters with the coats. She hands one to* **GINA**. *They exit.*)

JOHNNY. (*calls out*) And bring some Kool Aid!

(*Footage: dogs attacking peaceful Civil Rights marchers*)

Scene Seven

(ELENA arrives home from work, tired and worried. She finds ENRIQUE waiting for her.)

ENRIQUE. Why didn't you call me? I would have paid the light bill.

ELENA. I did once, but Mari answered and I hung up. After what happened… And you stopped coming over… I was embarrassed…

ENRIQUE. It was just a kiss, Elena…

ELENA. Then why did you stop coming over?

ENRIQUE. Because I thought I was… I didn't want to complicate your life, Elena. I…

ELENA. I'm sorry, I did that. I shouldn't have…

ENRIQUE. Don't be sorry.

(silence)

ELENA. Please don't disappear like that again.

ENRIQUE. I won't. I promise.

(ELENA sits.)

How long has he been gone?

ELENA. A month.

ENRIQUE. And he's not helping you pay for anything?

(She shakes her head "no.")

Hijo de su madre. (Son of his mother.)

ELENA. He has a girlfriend. My *comadre (good friend)* Alicia saw them together at the Riverside Ballroom. She said she looked like a floozy with her breasts sticking out in a real tight dress. That's the kind of women he likes. He always wanted me to dress like that.

ENRIQUE. That's not your style, *mi reina. (my queen)* You have more class than that.

ELENA. Who knows. Maybe he won't come back this time.

ENRIQUE. Do you want him to?

(She shrugs.)

ELENA. I don't know. I don't want the kids to be without their father.

(**ENRIQUE** *shakes his head.*)

ENRIQUE. *Es un pinche pendejo. Si tu fueras mi esposa, Elena…* (He's a fuckin' idiot. If you were my wife, Elena…)

(*She laughs.*)

ELENA. If I was your wife, what?

(**ENRIQUE** *looks at her.*)

You always say that, "If you were my wife…" Tell me. I really want to know what I'm missing out on.

(*He's caught off guard.* **ELENA** *waits for a response.*)

A ver. (Tell me.)

ENRIQUE. Well… I would buy you pretty clothes and send you to the beauty parlor once a week.

(**ELENA** *rolls her eyes and laughs.*)

And on the weekends we would go out so I could show you off to all my friends and we would dance together all night long. On Sundays we would take the kids on picnics and we would play the guitar and sing together. We would take them to Disneyland once a year.

(**ELENA** *smiles at the thought.*)

I would wake up every morning before you. I would sneak out of bed and make you coffee and serve you breakfast in bed. *(pause)* I would wake you up with kisses. I would love you the way you should be loved.

(*silence*)

ELENA. Let's do it, Enrique.

ENRIQUE. What?

ELENA. Let's pack up the kids and run away. Go far away from here…

(**ENRIQUE** *wonders if she is serious. He laughs.*)

ENRIQUE. *No estes bromiando conmigo, Elena. (Don't kid with me, Elena.)* You don't know how often I think about that night...

(He reaches for her hand. **BETTY** *calls from offstage:)*

BETTY. *(offstage)* Mom?

*(***ELENA*** *pulls her hand away from* **ENRIQUE**, *startled.* **BETTY** *and* **GINA** *enter, carrying their school books.* **GINA** *looks at* **ELENA** *and* **ENRIQUE** *suspiciously.)*

BETTY. Hi, *Tío Kiki.*

ENRIQUE. Hi, *m'ija...*

BETTY. We haven't seen you in ages.

ENRIQUE. Oh, I've been busy. With work and all...

(an awkward silence)

Ya me tengo que ir. (I have to go.)

ELENA. *Ándale pues. (Alright.)*

(He leaves.)

(Musical Interlude: "Love Hurts" soft and slow)*

Scene Eight

(**BETTY** *is in the bedroom. She can hear* **GINA** *throwing up in the bathroom.* **GINA** *enters. She looks green.*)

BETTY. When are you gonna tell Mom?

GINA. Never.

BETTY. You can't hide it forever.

GINA. I'm not gonna have it. I just need some money.

BETTY. You know why *Tía Mari* never had kids? She went to *Nogales* when she was young to get rid of her baby and she got real sick with an infection and they had to remove all of her female organs. Now she can't have kids.

GINA. Good. I hope that happens to me.

BETTY. No you don't. Gina, why don't you want to have kids?

GINA. Why would I? Give me one good reason.

(**BETTY** *can't think of one.*)

BETTY. You could die, you know.

GINA. What do you know about it?

BETTY. A lot. You know how they do it? They get a coat hanger and put it up in between your legs and it hurts real bad. And if the hanger's not clean…

GINA. Oh, shut up, this isn't the '40s. They have doctors in *Nogales* who know what they're doing.

BETTY. Not if you don't have any money. Yolanda's sister just had it done and that's how they did it.

GINA. Liar.

BETTY. I swear.

GINA. On what?

BETTY. On Mom's grave.

GINA. Mom's not dead.

BETTY. But, she will be one day. And I swear on that grave.

(**GINA** *goes back into the bathroom to throw up. We hear her gag.*)

BETTY. Ugh... That's disgusting!

GINA. *(offstage)* Shut up!

(*Musical interlude: "Humo en Los Ojos."**)

Scene Nine

(**ELENA** *is hanging laundry when* **MARI** *arrives. She is wearing a pretty dress with matching purse and shoes.*)

MARI. *Hola, Elena. (Hello, Elena.)*

(**ELENA** *is startled.*)

ELENA. *Mari. Qué milagro. (Mari. What a miracle.)*

MARI. I know. Big surprise, huh? I finally got out of the house. I hope it's okay. I should have called maybe…

ELENA. Of course, it's okay. *Siéntate. (Sit down.)*

(**MARI** *sits.*)

Do you want something? I have some *limonada (lemonade)* inside. *¿Quieres? (Want some?)*

MARI. *Bueno, un vasito, por favor. (Sure, a small glass, please.)*

(**ELENA** *enters the house.*)

Qué calor. (It's so hot.) This heat kills me. I never got used to it. In *Guadalajara* it got hot in the summer, but not like this.

(**ELENA** *returns with the lemonade.*)

Gracias, comadrita. (Thank you, little friend.)

(**MARI** *drinks.*)

Here, the heat is so heavy. You walk outside and it smothers you and you can't breath. Well, I can't. Maybe you're used to it. But, not me. *A mi, me mata. (It kills me.)*

(*She smiles.*)

¿Qué dramatica, verdad? (So dramatic, right?)

(*They laugh. Silence.*)

That's what Enrique says, that I'm too dramatic. I guess I am. But, I don't know how to be any other way. What do you think? Am I?

ELENA. Well… Maybe a little…

MARI. I know I am! I'm from *México.* We are very dramatic.

ELENA. My mother is from *México*. She used to threaten to commit suicide when we disobeyed her.

MARI. My mother did the same thing! *¡Ya vez! (You see!)*

(They laugh some more.)

ELENA. Are you feeling better, *Mari?*

*(**MARI** looks at **ELENA**.)*

MARI. Why? Did Enrique tell you that I was sick?

*(**ELENA** is not sure how to respond.)*

Did he? You can tell me the truth.

ELENA. Well, he mentioned something…

MARI. I am sick, Elena. My head is a mess. That's why the doctor wants me to try to get out of the house, because I just sit there thinking about things… And I'm trying. Today, Enrique woke me up with kisses like he always does. He brought me my coffee in bed and he made me promise that I would get out of the house. So, here I am. So, you see, *comadrita, (my friend)* you are part of the *tratamiento (treatment)* whether you know it or not. *(She drinks.)* In *San Francisco*, where my sister Flora lives, the breeze is so cool and it's not flat, like here. There are so many hills and the ocean and the Golden Gate Bridge… Just like in the movies.

*(She begins to cry. **ELENA** takes her hand.)*

ELENA. Mari, don't cry…

MARI. You know what I'm afraid of, Elena?

ELENA. What?

MARI. I'm afraid that Enrique will get tired of me and the way I am… I try to be happy, *pero siento el corazon pesado (my heart is so heavy)* and I can't. I wish I could be like you. Your life is so… Well, Carlos, he comes and goes and he… *(She stops.)* I'm sorry… I should shut up.

ELENA. It's okay, *comadre, (my friend,)* you can say it.

MARI. It's just that you seem so happy, even if… things are not so good in your life. How do you do that?

(ELENA shrugs.)

ELENA. I don't know. You learn to make the best of things, I guess. That's the way I was brought up.

MARI. That's the way Enrique is. Always content with life. And lately, he's so happy, he sings and whistles and tries to look real nice when he goes to work... And my crazy mind gets going and I get afraid that he'll meet somebody, you know. Someone who... who isn't... *safada, (nuts,)* like me. If that happened, I don't know what I would do. I would probably end up in the nut house or I would probably die. *(She laughs.)* Oh my God. I'm like a bad *novela.*

(silence)

He's always talking about you and the kids... He likes you all so much. I know he talks to you, Elena. Has he said anything? Anything you think I should know?

ELENA. No.

MARI. Are you sure?

(ELENA doesn't know what to say.)

ELENA. Yes, there is something you should know...

(MARI waits.)

Enrique loves you with all his heart. He's a good man. He'll never leave you, Mari. Never.

Scene Ten

(CARLOS *arrives, looking lost and disheveled. He puts down his suit case.* JOHNNY *enters.*)

CARLOS. *M'ijo. (My son.)*

(*He opens his arm for* JOHNNY *to embrace him.* JOHNNY *hesitates.*)

JOHNNY. Dad?

CARLOS. Come here, son.

(JOHNNY *embraces* CARLOS, *halfheartedly.*)

I missed you.

JOHNNY. Does Mom know you're back?

CARLOS. Not yet. Is she mad?

JOHNNY. What do you think? Where were you? You didn't call or anything.

CARLOS. I know. I missed you all so much. My home, my kids.

JOHNNY. What about that other woman?

CARLOS. What other woman?

JOHNNY. The one everybody saw you with, Dad.

(*pause*)

CARLOS. It was nothing. Didn't mean anything...

(ELENA *enters.*)

ELENA. When did you get back?

CARLOS. Just now.

(*He tries to kiss* ELENA *but she pulls away.* GINA, BETTY *and* BOBBY *enter.*)

Elena, I swear. I'll never do it again.

ELENA. How many times...

CARLOS. Elena, I swear. I swear on my mother's grave.

ELENA. Oh, stop!

GINA. Don't take him back, Mom. Not after everything he's done to you?

CARLOS. Gina…

GINA. He abandoned us to be with another woman, Mom! Are you that stupid?

CARLOS. Don't talk to your mother like that!

GINA. What are you gonna do, Dad? Hit me? Go ahead!

ELENA. Gina, stop! *(**ELENA** stands between **GINA** and **CARLOS**.)*

*(to **CARLOS**)* You can't leave and come back and expect us to greet you with open arms.

CARLOS. What do you want? To raise the kids alone? Without a father? They need me.

GINA. We don't need you!

JOHNNY. Be quiet, Gina!

CARLOS. You see, look at them, they're out of control.

ELENA. We were doing just fine…

CARLOS. I swear, I'll change. Elena, please? What do I have to do, beg you? I will. I will. I'll get on my knees, look. I'm sorry…

*(He gets on his knees in front of **ELENA**.)*

ELENA. Stop, Carlos, get up.

GINA. Oh, God! Don't fall for it, Mom!

BETTY. Stop it, Gina, he said he's sorry!

BOBBY. Shut up, Betty!

*(**GINA** looks at her siblings.)*

GINA. I can't believe you guys! He abandoned us. Don't you remember? We were so hungry we had to steal food.

*(None of them answers except for **BOBBY**.)*

BOBBY. I remember.

GINA. *(to **CARLOS**)* We stole food, Dad, so that we could eat! Because you were screwing around and didn't give a shit!

ELENA. Gina!

BETTY. Shut up, Gina! Shut up! Give Dad a chance. You're
   not perfect. She's not perfect, Mom. She's in trouble.
   She's gonna have a baby!

   *(**BETTY** is sorry as soon as she says it. **ELENA** looks at
   GINA.)*

ELENA. What? No, Gina…

GINA. You liar! You liar!

   *(She runs out. **BETTY** runs out after **GINA**.)*

BETTY. Gina…

GINA. *(offstage)* Stay away from me, you little bitch!

   (Music: "You'll Lose A Good Thing")*

   *(**ELENA** is devastated by the news about **GINA**. **CARLOS**
   embraces **ELENA** and she lets him this time.)*

CARLOS. ¿Ya ves? *(You see?)* You need me here. And I need
   you…so much.

   (They go into the house.)

---

*Please see Music Use Note on page 3

Scene Eleven

(Music: "You'll Lose A Good Thing")

*(**GINA** sings the first four lines.*)*

(Song continues under the scene.*)

*(Lights up on **RUDY**, in uniform.)*

RUDY. Dear Gina, I'll be home in one week. I told my Sergeant that I want to marry you and that we're going to have a baby. We've made all the arrangements. I can't wait to be with you. I love you more than anything or anybody in the world. Yours forever, Love, Rudy. SWAK, sealed with a kiss.

*(**GINA** is in her room. She has a pill bottle in her hand.)*

*(**GINA** sings the next seven lines.*)*

*(**GINA** opens the bottle and empties all the pills into her hand. She gulps them all down with a Coca-Cola.)*

*(**RUDY** sings the last verse of "You'll Lose A Good Thing"*)*

*(**BETTY** enters and finds **GINA** unconscious.)*

BETTY. Gina! Gina! Mom! Mom!

*(**RUDY** sings the last lines of "You'll Lose A Good Thing"*)*

(an ambulance siren)

---

*Please see Music Use Note on page 3

Scene Twelve

(**GINA** *is in a hospital bed, weak and groggy.* **ELENA** *strokes her head.*)

ELENA. I talked to *Nana* and she says you can go stay with her until you have the baby. Do you want to do that?

GINA. Yeah.

ELENA. Then you can decide what you want to do.

GINA. Why don't we all go, Mom? What do you have here?

(**ELENA** *doesn't respond.* **GINA** *figures it out.*)

Is Dad back?

ELENA. For now.

GINA. He's never gonna change. He's just gonna leave again.

ELENA. If he does, your *Tío Kiki*...

GINA. *Tío Kiki?* If you think he's going to leave my *Tia Mari* for you, you're wrong.

ELENA. What? That's not what I think. Why would you say that?

GINA. I saw you with him. I saw you with him the night of the dance. I saw *Tío Kiki* kissing you in bed...

ELENA. No, we didn't do what you think. I mean, yes, we kissed, but nothing else happened, I swear to you...

(*silence*)

GINA. Why do you take Dad back? Why, Mom?

ELENA. I do it for you. So, you'll have a father.

GINA. No you don't. You do it for yourself. It's what you want, Mom, not us. It always is.

(**GINA** *turns away from* **ELENA**. **ELENA** *leaves.*)

Scene Thirteen

(As **ELENA** *leaves the hospital, she runs into* **ENRIQUE.**)

ENRIQUE. How's Gina?

ELENA. She's upset. But, she'll be okay.

ENRIQUE. So, you let him come back?

ELENA. Yes.

ENRIQUE. Why, Elena?

ELENA. Old habits are hard to break, I guess.

ENRIQUE. But, I thought... You said you wanted us to run away...

ELENA. I let myself dream for a minute.

(*silence*)

You don't know...how much I need your friendship, your company. Sometimes, it's the only thing I have to hold on to. And it's not about what we talked about or what we almost did that night. It's about more than that. But, things don't turn out the way we think they will. You have a wife. What kind of a woman makes a husband leave his wife?

(**ENRIQUE** *looks at her.*)

ENRIQUE. Elena...

ELENA. Please, go home to Mari. Go home to your wife. She needs you more than I do.

(**ELENA** *walks away.*)

(*SONG: "Qué Seas Feliz"**)

(**ENRIQUE** *sings seven lines.**)

(*He exits.*)

---

*Please see Music Use Note on page 3

Scene Fourteen

(**BETTY** *sits on the bed next to* **GINA**. **BOBBY** *and*
JOHNNY *sit on the floor next to the bed.* **GINA** *opens her*
eyes, sees her siblings and closes them again.)

GINA. What do you want?

BETTY. We just want to make sure you're okay, Gina.

JOHNNY. Yeah. Do you need anything?

GINA. Yes, I need you to go away.

BETTY. Be nice, Gina.

GINA. Okay, don't go away.

BOBBY. Gina... Did you really want to die?

BETTY. Of course not. It was an accident, wasn't it Gina?

GINA. Yeah, I swallowed twenty sleeping pills by accident.

BETTY. But, you didn't lose the baby.

BOBBY. That's good.

JOHNNY. Yeah.

(**GINA** *turns away from them.*)

BETTY. You got a letter from Rudy.

BOBBY. We read it!

BETTY. Because you were in the hospital.

JOHNNY. He's coming home and he wants to marry you.

GINA. You're lucky I don't feel well or I'd kick your ass!

(*silence*)

BETTY. What are we gonna do, Gina?

GINA. About what?

BETTY. About the baby...

GINA. I don't know. I had a plan and that went to shit.

JOHNNY. We're gonna have it...

(**GINA** *looks at* **JOHNNY**.)

GINA. We? Oh, Dad's gonna love that.

JOHNNY. Who cares what Dad wants. I don't.

BOBBY. I don't either.

(**GINA** *looks at* **JOHNNY.**)

JOHNNY. He cheats on Mom.

BETTY. Johnny...

JOHNNY. He does, Betty! Everybody saw him with that woman! I mean, he practically told me.

BETTY. I don't want Dad to leave! I don't want to live like that again, without food and light. I don't like being poor...

BOBBY. Shut up, you big baby!

BETTY. Well, I don't...

GINA. He's not gonna leave, Betty, I am.

(*They look at her.*)

I'm going to Los Angeles to live with *Nana.*

BETTY. Gina, no.

GINA. I have to. Dad won't let me stay here like this.

BOBBY. Dad should leave, we don't need him.

JOHNNY. Don't worry, Gina, we'll figure this out.

(*Footage: President and Mrs. Kennedy at LULAC dinner in Houston, Texas, October 21, 1963*)

Scene Fifteen

(ELENA *arrives home and enters the kitchen. She calls out.*)

ELENA. Kiki? *(no answer)* Kiki?

(CARLOS *enters.*)

Oh, it's you. Where's Kiki? I saw his car outside.

CARLOS. It's mine now. I bought it from him.

ELENA. You did?

CARLOS. Dirt cheap. He says he'll buy another one in San Francisco...

ELENA. San Francisco?

CARLOS. He's moving to San Francisco with *Mari,* so she can be close to her sister. You mean he didn't tell you?

ELENA. No.

CARLOS. They left early this morning.

(ELENA *sits down, shocked.*)

(*He goes to her, embraces her and tries to comfort her. She begins to cry.*)

Hey, what's going on?

(*He wipes her tears from her face, kisses her cheek and* ELENA *let's down her guard.*)

ELENA. I can't believe he would leave me... *(She catches herself.)* ...not without saying goodbye.

CARLOS. *(He puts two and two together...)* Are you in love with him? What did you do? Did you sleep with Kiki? Did you?

(ELENA *doesn't answer.*)

Answer me!

ELENA. No! What if I did? You sleep with other women, don't you?

(*The kids look at* ELENA *in shock.*)

CARLOS. ¡Hija de tu chingada madre! *(You fucking bitch!)*

(He moves toward **ELENA**.*)*

GINA. Stop, Dad!

(She pushes him away.)

CARLOS. Get your hands off of me!

(He goes for his belt. **BOBBY** *steps in front of* **GINA**.*)*

BOBBY. No, Dad, don't!

*(***CARLOS*** pushes* **BOBBY** *out of the way and* **JOHNNY** *steps in.)*

JOHNNY. You can't hit us anymore, Dad! You can't!

*(***JOHNNY*** pushes* **CARLOS**, *hard! Finally* **ELENA** *stands up.)*

ELENA. Stop it! Stop it!

(They all look at her.)

Maybe I do love him! Maybe I do… But, not the way you think. It's not about sex or lust or possessiveness or jealousy, but about trust and goodness and giving and respect…

CARLOS. Do you expect me to believe that?

ELENA. No, I don't! Because you'll never understand, you can't. And I really don't care if you do or not. *(from her depths:)* Now, get out! Get the hell out of my house! Get out and leave me and my children alone!

(He looks at the kids.)

CARLOS. You want me to leave?

ELENA. Yes!

CARLOS. I'll never come back. I mean it.

ELENA. Good, don't come back. Please, don't ever come back.

*(***CARLOS*** goes for his coat.)*

CARLOS. Come on, Johnny, let's go. You're coming with me.

(**JOHNNY** *looks at* **CARLOS** *then at* **ELENA**. *He doesn't move.*)

CARLOS. Come on.

(**JOHNNY** *doesn't move.*)

I said, come on.

JOHNNY. No, Dad. I'm staying. I'm staying with Mom.

(**CARLOS** *looks at* **BETTY**. *She is crying.*)

CARLOS. Betty, *m'ija,* *(my daughter,)* come here.

(**BETTY** *shakes her head and cries.*)

BETTY. No.

(**CARLOS** *looks at* **GINA**, **BOBBY**, **ELENA**. *Nobody's flinching.*)

JOHNNY. You heard Mom. You gotta leave. Go on, Dad. Get out.

(**CARLOS** *looks at* **ELENA**.)

CARLOS. Remember, you did this, not me!

(*He exits.*)

(*The phone rings.*)

Scene Sixteen

(**BETTY** *is on the phone with* **JACK.** *JFK silhouette appears.*)

BETTY. Jack?

JACK. Yes, Betty, it's me…

BETTY. Where are you?

JACK. I'm in Texas, Betty…

BETTY. Texas?

JACK. Yeah. Hee haw! *(He chuckles.)* In Houston with Mexican Americans, just like you, Betty. And there is a mariachi band playing Spanish songs. And tomorrow we'll be in a parade in Dallas…

BETTY. Well, I'll be watching…

JACK. It's good to know you will be, Betty. But, right now I'm dealing with Southeast Asia…

BETTY. Southeast Asia?

JACK. Yes, Betty, there's a small country there called Vietnam. Actually, there's two: North Vietnam, currently run by communists and South Vietnam that, well, don't tell anyone but…

BETTY. I promise…

JACK. We just helped overthrow their government and replaced it with a military regime.

BETTY. What? Oh, God, Jack, don't you ever learn?

JACK. What's that, Betty?

BETTY. Why do you have to keep sticking your nose into everybody's business, geez!

JACK. Betty, are you alright?

BETTY. No, I'm not! My sister is expecting a baby and she tried to commit suicide and my uncle moved to *San Francisco* and my dad thinks my mom had an affair and my mom kicked my dad out and we're losing the house because we can't pay the house payment and, well, my life is a big mess.

JACK. Now, now, Betty. Things will get better, don't you worry. Families are always hard to deal with. One day when we have time, I'll tell you about my family and all of our ups and downs.

BETTY. No you won't...

JACK. What?

BETTY. You're never going to tell me about your family, Jack...

JACK. Of course, I will...

BETTY. Jack, let's be honest here, okay?

(*silence*)

JACK. Alright...

BETTY. This thing we have... This thing between you and me. It's not real. And, well... I think... I think we have to stop. I mean, you have a wife, Jack... And, well... We can pretend that everything is hunky, dory... But, we both know it isn't. This...life thing... It's really hard... And, I have to figure it out. So, I think it's best if we don't talk anymore. Okay?

(*silence*)

Jack?

JACK. I'm here, Betty... And, I understand. I'll miss you, Betty.

(*She cries.*)

BETTY. ...and I'll miss you. Goodbye, Jack.

JACK. Goodbye, Betty.

(**BETTY** *hangs up.*)

(*Footage: President Kennedy and Jackie arriving in Dallas*)

Scene Seventeen

(**BETTY** *is watching the presidential motorcade on
television:*)

TV VOICE. The president's car is now turning on to Elm
street and it will be only a matter of minutes before
he arrives at the Trademark. It appears as though
something has happened in the motorcade route..
stand by something has happened at the motorcade
route...

(*Footage: Walter Cronkite*)

WALTER CRONKITE. From Dallas, Texas, the flash apparently
official: President Kennedy died at 1 p.m. Central
Standard Time, 2:00 Eastern Standard Time, some
thirty-eightminutes ago.

(*pause as* **CRONKITE** *fights back tears, then regains his
composure*)

BETTY. Mom... Mom... No. No!

Scene Eighteen

(**RUDY**, *in uniform, and* **GINA** *are sitting underneath the dead weeping willow tree.*)

GINA. Why would you want to marry me?

RUDY. I want to take care of you. You're always taking care of everybody. Let me take care of you and our baby.

GINA. It's probably going to be born retarded or deformed because I took all those pills.

RUDY. Don't say that. It doesn't matter. I don't care, Gina. It will be our little retarded and deformed baby and we will love him or her because it will be ours.

GINA. How come you're so good?

RUDY. I'm not. I'm not good. I just know I need you and I can't live without you.

(*He kisses her and she kisses him back.*)

GINA. Rudy, I want to be honest.

RUDY. I know, you can't help it.

GINA. I don't love you...yet. But, if you're the kind of man, I think you are, I think I will. You're not like most men and I like that about you. All I can say is I'll try to be a good mother...and I'll try to be a good wife..

RUDY. I know you will be, Gina. There's no doubt in my mind. I can't believe my baby is going to be born in Los Angeles! President Johnson is shipping me out, but as soon as I get back I'll be there, right on your doorstep.

(*They embrace.*)

If the baby's a boy, I want to name him John Fitzgerald, after our late president. Is that alright with you?

GINA. Okay. And *Guadalupe* after my *Tata.*

RUDY. John Fitzgerald Guadalupe? (*pause*) I like it.

GINA. And if it's a girl, we'll name her *Esperanza*, after my *Nana.*

RUDY. Esperanza… Hope. That's good.

*(He puts his hand on her stomach and beams. **GINA** shakes her head and smiles.)*

Scene Nineteen

(Footage of President Kennedy's Funeral continues through scene.)

*(**ELENA** and the kids are sitting in the living room with suitcases, dressed and waiting for a cab. The whole family is in mourning for the president.)*

ELENA. He was so young and handsome.

BOBBY. And he was a Catholic.

JOHNNY. That's why *Nana* liked him.

ELENA. Poor *Nana*. She had so much hope for him.

*(Silence. **BETTY** cries and **ELENA** strokes her head.)*

Shh.. Shhh…

JOHNNY. Mom, as soon as we get to California, I'm gonna find a job so we can get our own house for when Gina has the baby.

*(**ELENA** looks at **JOHNNY**.)*

ELENA. Okay, *m'ijo. (my son)*

(Music: "Mr. Sandman")*

*(**GINA** sings the first line.*)*

*(**BETTY** sings the second line.*)*

*(**JOHNNY** sings the third line.*)*

*(**ALL** sing the fourth line.*)*

*(**BOBBY** sings the fifth and sixth line.*)*

*(**ALL** sing the next four lines.*)*

(Footage: Jon Jon Kennedy salutes his father's casket)

(Lights fade.)

---

*Please see Music Use Note on page 3

End of Play

Charity

Part III

(2005)

CHARITY: PART III OF A MEXICAN TRILOGY was first produced by the Latino Theater Company in Los Angeles, CA on May 5, 2012 at the Los Angeles Theatre Center. The performance was directed by Jose Luis Valenzuela, with sets by Francois-Pierre Couture, lights and projections by Cameron Mock, costumes by Carlos Brown, sound by John Zalewski, choreography by Urbanie Lucero, and original music by Marcos Loya. The Production Stage Manager was Henry "Heno" Fernandez. The cast was as follows:

ESPERANZA	Ofelia Medina
GINA	Evelina Fernandez
VALENTINA	Esperanza America
RUDY	Rudy Ramos
JUAN FRANCISCO	Jonathan Cruz
EMILIANO	Sam Golzari
BETTY	Lucy Rodriguez
BOBBY	Geoffrey Rivas
SILVESTRE	Sal Lopez
JOHNNY	Sal Lopez

CHARACTERS

GINA – 50s, mourns her son's death in the Iraq war and is obsessed with Pope John Paul II funeral services.

RUDY – 50s, Gina's husband, is torn between his own mourning and his new fondness of Juan Francisco.

VALENTINA – 20, Gina's only daughter.

EMILIANO – 22, Gina's dead son, talks to Esperanza in the upstairs bedroom.

SILVESTRE – 50s, Esperanza's dead husband, comes to take Esperanza to the great beyond.

JUAN FRANCISCO – 20s, an unexpected relative who arrives from Mexico in search of the American dream.

JOHNNY – 50s, Gina's brother, a Vietnam vet, still suffers from the horrors of the war.

BOBBY – 50s, Gina's brother, a gay hair salon owner, gives Juan Francisco a job.

BETTY – 50s, Gina's sister, still hasn't found the right man. She shares her love problems with Esperanza.

SETTING

Los Angeles, California

TIME

2005

Prologue

("Mr. Sandman" plays softly as lights come up on
GINA, *now in her 50s, enters carrying a letter-size*
envelope. Lights reveal a middle class two-story Los
Angeles home. A table sits center stage with a sofa stage
right. **ESPERANZA**, *now over 100 years old, with long*
white hair, wanders through the house in a long, white
nightgown. She makes her way up the stairs into her
upstairs room while **GINA** *looks at the envelope for a long*
while and then sets it down on the table. She sits down
on the couch to watch television. **ESPERANZA** *lies down*
in her bed. She dreams... Images of the 20th century
appear: the Mexican revolution of 1910, the great
depression, WWI, WWII, the Korean War, Vietnam,
Pancho Villa, Emiliano Zapata, FDR, Truman,
Eisenhower, JFK, MLK, RFK, the Chicano Moratorium,
Vietnam, President Johnson, Nixon, Desert Storm, 9/11,
all in an instant.)

(Everything stops. Bells toll.)

*(***ESPERANZA** *sits up. She breathes hard. She is alone,*
frightened and confused.)

ESPERANZA. ¿Gina? ¿Gina? *¡Contéstame, cabrona! ¡Ven, tengo*
que decirte algo! (Answer me, damn it! I have something to
tell you.)

(Footage: announcement of the death of Pope John Paul
II)

(Lights come up on **GINA** *on the couch watching the*
coverage of the Pope's death.)

(offstage) ¡Gina! ¡Gina!

*(***GINA** *doesn't respond. Her daughter,* **VALENTINA**, *20'*
enters with books and a laptop in her arms.)

VALENTINA. Mom, *Nana's* calling you.

GINA. Shhh… I'm watching this.

VALENTINA. But…

GINA. I was just up there. She calls me and I go up and she forgets what she wanted to say.

VALENTINA. But, Mom, isn't ignoring her elderly abuse?

GINA. No. She refuses to die and we have to take care of her. That's abuse.

VALENTINA. Inconsiderate maybe, but not abuse.

GINA. That's your opinion.

ESPERANZA. *(offstage)* ¡Guillermina!

VALENTINA. Mom…

GINA. Shhh… Let me watch this.

ESPERANZA. *(offstage)* ¡Gina!

> *(Lights come up on the* **ESPERANZA**. *She is smoking a cigarette.)*

> *Que te tengo que decir algo.* I have to tell you something… Look, if you don't come, who cares? I already forgot what I was going to say. Something important. But what?

> *(confused)* I don't remember.

> *(She laughs.)*

> Don't you see that I'm not dead yet? And don't feel like it, either. What for? To be with those who have already gone? What will I say when they ask about my life? What?

> *(She takes another drag on her cigarette.)*

> *Qué vida tan larga…* (What a long life…)

> I've seen so many things, known a whole bunch of people, sung a whole lot of songs, danced a thousand dances… I've greeted a million suns, bid farewell to millions of moons and I have contemplated the stars and the planets… I've loved, I've hated, I've kissed, I've cried…not too much, but I have cried. I cried

when my mother died and when my father died... I cried when my baby girl, Amada, died... I cried for years and I never thought I would be rid of that pain, but yes... It's not that it passes... you just get used to it.

(She takes another drag.)

Yes, I've cried... But, more than anything I've enjoyed life and that's why I'm still here, I think. Around twenty or maybe twenty five years ago... I must have been, well let's see, around eighty years old back then. I thought I was going to die, of old age, because I didn't feel ill. I wasn't sick, I wasn't crazy...yet.

(She laughs.)

En ese entonces me preparé para morirme ... I prepared myself to die... I began giving away my things, I didn't have much...some gold earrings that had belonged to my mother, may she be with God in heaven, my rosaries, some embroidered handkerchiefs...

I began to tell my loved ones the things I needed to tell them before I left... I thanked them... I asked them for forgiveness... I forgave them... I told them that they were good... that I was proud of them... I kissed them and I remembered when they were children... old women who I had raised in my arms... I gave them life, I fed them from my own breasts, I bathed them, taught them, I spanked them too because some of them were rascals...

Old wrinkled women with children, grandchildren and great grandchildren and I remembered the moment each one of them arrived on this earth and when they filled their lungs with their first breath of life. I remembered their first cry, their first sigh, I remembered the first time I held them up to my face and the scent that only a baby has, their skin like silk, their sweet and innocent breath...the sweet moment when a child cries with love because he wants his mothers arms and breast because he is so in love with her...and she in love with her child. Poor men, no?

They don't know what it's like to feel the movement of a child inside of your womb... That profound love that a mother feels for her child. What am I saying? Poor men? No!

And they died one by one. The first one to die was my oldest daughter, *Fe (Faith)*. It hurt so much. And then, *Caridad (Charity)* and I realized they were all going to die and that I wasn't. And that's how it happened. My youngest daughter, Elena, died and that's why I'm here in the house of my granddaughter, Gina...

(She yells!)

¡Gina! ¡Gina! ¡Hija de la tiznada! (Daughter of darkness!)

(Sound: the High Mass)

ACT ONE

Scene One

(Footage: the Pope lying in state)

*(**GINA** sits in front of the television. **VALENTINA** sits at the table at her laptop.)*

VALENTINA. Mom, why are we watching this?

GINA. Because he's the Pope.

VALENTINA. And?

*(**GINA** gives her a disapproving look.)*

GINA. And what?

VALENTINA. You know I'm not a fan of organized religion and neither are you. Since when are you so into the Pope?

GINA. Since he's dead.

VALENTINA. We aren't real Catholics, Mom. You know Miliano and I only made our sacraments because of Grandma Elena. We're non-practicing Catholics and that's okay. There're millions of us.

GINA. Okay, so what's your point?

*(**VALENTINA** sits next to **GINA** on the couch.)*

VALENTINA. My point is I don't know why you're watching this because…

GINA. He was against the war.

VALENTINA. What?

GINA. The Pope. He was against the war. If they would have listened to him… Now, let me watch this in peace.

VALENTINA. Maybe he was against the war, but…

GINA. *¡Ya!* That's enough.

VALENTINA. See! Nobody can express their opinion around here! Don't I have any rights?

GINA. No, you don't! Not in my house.

VALENTINA. Mom, that is so wrong.

GINA. Okay, I'm wrong. So what?

(**VALENTINA** *reaches for the envelope on the table.*)

Don't touch that! Leave it there!

(**VALENTINA** *puts it down.*)

VALENTINA. Sorry! Geez!

(*She exits in frustration as* **GINA** *continues to watch.*)

(*Music plays. Footage: the Pope's services.*)

Scene Two

(Lights up on the upstairs bedroom where **ESPERANZA** *is smoking, lying on her bed like a beauty queen. To the left of her bed is a chair and a table with knick knacks, photos, a rosary and a bottle of tequila.)*

ESPERANZA. Who would have thought we'd have a Polish Pope! *Y tan buenote que estaba. (And he was so handsome.)*

(She laughs. **VALENTINA** *enters.)*

VALENTINA. Who you talking to, *Nana?*

ESPERANZA. To myself, who else?

VALENTINA. What happened to your guardian angel?

ESPERANZA. Ah, I gave him the day off. He's getting old... So, I'm talking to myself because nobody else talks to me.

VALENTINA. I do.

ESPERANZA. What's your name again?

VALENTINA. You know my name. Stop faking.

*(***ESPERANZA*** laughs.)*

ESPERANZA. What happened? You fought with your mother again?

VALENTINA. No...

ESPERANZA. Yes, you did. You can't lie to me. I know when you're lying. Your voice goes up like...

(She imitates her.)

"No..." Just like your mother, and her mother...

VALENTINA. And you?

ESPERANZA. That's right. Your great grandmother. We don't know how to lie and it's a curse from hell. We have to tell the truth and we live with that burden. I've seen women live their whole life without ever telling the truth and they live a very comfortable life. Not us, *hija,* our voice betrays us. *Qué pinche suerte, ¿no? (What fuckin' luck, huh?)*

VALENTINA. I thought being honest was a virtue.

(ESPERANZA *laughs.*)

ESPERANZA. Who told you that? Is it a virtue to shout out hurtful words to someone you love and not be able to stop yourself? Is it a virtue to tell your husband to go to hell? It's not a virtue, it's a curse! A *pinche (fucking)* curse from hell!

(*She wipes her tears and recovers all at once.*)

So, what happened? You told her the truth *y se enojó, o ¿qué?* (*and she got angry or what?*)

VALENTINA. You know she's always angry. I asked her why she's glued to the TV watching the Pope's funeral...

ESPERANZA. *Tan chulo estaba...* (*He was so handsome...*) Why did the handsome ones always become priests? Not anymore, but in my day...

VALENTINA. *Nana*... were in love with a priest?

ESPERANZA. No! (*pause*) Well, just one... *Bien chulo que estaba, el cabrón.* (*He was a handsome son of a gun.*) I would go to mass five times a day just to receive communion from him. My heart would pound in anticipation of the holy eucharist.

VALENTINA. *Nana*, that's kind of kinky. And when was your day, exactly?

(*She motions for* VALENTINA *to help her up.* VALENTINA *does.*)

ESPERANZA. *Pues,* (*Well,*) let me see... What year is it now?

VALENTINA. 2005...

ESPERANZA. Another century? Well, let's put it this way, *hija.* (*daughter*) This is my third one. I was born in the 19th, lived in the 20th, and I will die in the 21st... maybe.

VALENTINA. There's some big bets on that.

ESPERANZA. *¿De veras?* (*Really?*) Well, let me give you a betting tip. *La yerba mala nunca muere.* (*Bad weeds never die.*)

VALENTINA. *¿La yerba mala? Nana*, you're not bad!

ESPERANZA. Not anymore. I'm too old. When you're young you act out. When you're old you act in. Don't think you know everything that goes on in this head of mine.

VALENTINA. Hardly. Everybody thinks you're crazy. But, I don't.

ESPERANZA. You don't?

VALENTINA. No. Eccentric, yes. Dramatic, very. Yearning to be the center of attention, absolutely. But, crazy… no.

ESPERANZA. But, don't tell anybody, *hija.* I like them to think I'm crazy. Can we keep it our little secret?

VALENTINA. That you are a very manipulative old woman? I guess.

(silence)

ESPERANZA. Don't worry. Your mother's anger will pass. She lost her only son. She has a right to question God and his motives. Let her grieve. Let her lash out at him. He deserves it sometimes.
Pinche guerra, m'ija. (Fucking war, my daughter.) Listen to the voice of experience. War sucks! *Como dicen ustedes. (Like you say.)* But, it does. It sucks the life out of the young, the innocent, it sucks the love out of life, it sucks the faith and hope out of humanity. Young people die and if they don't, they come back… *dados a la chingada. (all fucked up)*

VALENTINA. My Dad went to war and he's okay.

ESPERANZA. Who says he's okay? They're never okay. Some people hide it better than others. Look at your uncle, Johnny… *Tan chulo y talentoso que era. ¿Y ahora? Míralo. (He was so handsome and talented. And now? Look at him.)*

VALENTINA. My Mom says it's just an excuse…

*(**ESPERANZA** stands.)*

ESPERANZA. Your Mom doesn't know! Have compassion for him, *m'ija. (my daughter)* He's damaged. *Pobrecito m'ijo. (My poor grandson.)* Now you all look down at him like your *caca (shit)* doesn't smell.

VALENTINA. My Dad doesn't look down on him..

ESPERANZA. Because he knows... He knows... *Pinche gobierno. (Fucking government.)* All the governments, every one I've lived through... They think they can make peace by making war! Isn't that the stupidest thing you've ever heard? And yet, it happens over and over again.

(She looks at a corner in her room and starts walking toward it. **SILVESTRE**, *is standing there, but only* **ESPERANZA** *can see him.)*

(to **SILVESTRE***)* Why? Would you ask God why?

*(***VALENTINA** *looks at the corner.)*

VALENTINA. *Nana,* who are you talking to?

ESPERANZA. My guardian angel. He's back.

*(***VALENTINA** *smiles.)*

VALENTINA. Faker.

(She begins to exit down the stairs.)

ESPERANZA. No, wait! I have something I have to tell you.

VALENTINA. What?

ESPERANZA. I... I can't remember, but it's important.

VALENTINA. If you, remember, holler, okay?

(She exits. **ESPERANZA** *calls out after her.)*

ESPERANZA. Tell your mother I need papers for my cigarettes!

(The High Mass sounds continue from the TV.)

(Footage: images of Pope John Paul II's funeral)

Scene Three

(**GINA** *sits in front of the television in the livingroom.*
VALENTINA *enters.*)

VALENTINA. Mom, did you know that *Nana* was in love with
a priest when she was young?

GINA. Don't pay any attention. She doesn't know what she's
saying.

(*Suddenly* **VALENTINA** *is overcome by love and
understanding for her mother. She goes to her, hugs her
and kisses her.* **VALENTINA** *lies down on the couch with
her head on* **GINA**'s *lap.* **GINA** *strokes her head. They
watch the TV for a sec.*)

VALENTINA. I guess the Pope was kind of likable. I do like
his little Santa suit...

GINA. Stop!

VALENTINA. Just kidding, Mom. I know, he was against the
war and...

GINA. ...and he was handsome, too.

VALENTINA. You too? What is it with the women in our
family and priests? Attracted to the Pope, isn't that a
sin?

GINA. I wasn't attracted to him. I just think he was
handsome, that's all.

VALENTINA. *Nana* says all the good looking guys became
priests in her day.

GINA. Whenever that was.

(*silence*)

VALENTINA. Do you think about Miliano every minute of
every day?

GINA. (*She nods*) Uh huh.

VALENTINA. Me, too... I wish I believed in heaven so that I
could believe that I'll see him again.

(*Sound cue: prayers from the television*)

GINA. I want to say a rosary for your brother.

VALENTINA. A rosary? Are you serious? Do you even know how?

(**GINA** stands.)

GINA. Of course I do! I mean kind of… Can you Google it or something?

VALENTINA. Why don't you just ask *Nana*, she'll tell you how.

GINA. She only knows it in Spanish… Besides, I don't want her to know that I don't remember…

VALENTINA. She'll be pissed, huh?

GINA. And don't run up there and snitch on me either.

VALENTINA. I won't…

(**GINA** looks at her.)

I won't!

(**VALENTINA** goes to her laptop.)

GINA. I know the prayers: Our Fathers and Hail Marys. I just don't know the in between stuff.

(**VALENTINA** is reading from the internet:)

VALENTINA. Okay, here we go… (reads) "How to pray the Rosary: 1) Make the Sign of the Cross and say the "Apostles' Creed."

GINA. Which one is that?

VALENTINA. Let's see here… "I believe in God, the Father Almighty…"

GINA. Oh, yeah. I know that one: I believe in God the Father Almighty, Creator of heaven and earth…

VALENTINA. You forgot to make the sign of the cross and don't you need the beads?

(as her voice trails off…)

Scene Four

(Lights up on the ESPERANZA *talking to* GINA's *dead son,* EMILIANO, *20s. He wears a military uniform and holds his hat in his hand.)*

EMILIANO. It's not bad, *Nana.* It's… How should I put it? It's peaceful.

ESPERANZA. Peaceful? Sounds boring.

(He chuckles.)

EMILIANO. It isn't boring.

(pause)

It's… I can't really describe it in this life's terms. I can only say… You'll love it. When you get there. I'm not rushing you or anything.

ESPERANZA. You know better.

EMILIANO. That's right. *(silence)* Help my mom, *Nana.* Tell her to let it go. To let me go. Tell her to live again.

ESPERANZA. She won't listen to me. She thinks I'm crazy. *(She catches herself.)* And I am. In case you're wondering. *(She looks at him and sighs.)* Ay, Emiliano… *(pause)* Why did your mother name you Emiliano?

EMILIANO. After Zapata, you know that.

ESPERANZA. I know that. But, why after all these years? What the hell can Emiliano Zapata mean to her?

EMILIANO. They're from the '70s, you know. Reaching back to your roots, embracing your cultural heritage and all that. That's why she named Valentina, Valentina. She said you used to sing an old revolutionary song.

ESPERANZA. I did not!

EMILIANO. My Mom doesn't lie.

ESPERANZA. Well, maybe I did. *(She hums.)* "Valentina, Valentina…" Yes, maybe I did. It's a pretty name, Valentina. *Pero (But) ¿Emiliano?* She should have named you Leandro, after my father. Now, that's a beautiful name, Leandro.

EMILIANO. Leandro. That's not a hero's name.

ESPERANZA. Don't say that! He was a hero. He was a hero to me!

EMILIANO. Sorry.

ESPERANZA. Don't say sorry unless you mean it!

My father was a man. A gentleman. Tall, educated, proud. He loved me so much! And I broke his heart. I broke his heart when I ran away with your great grandfather. When you're young, you don't think about anyone but yourself. You fall in love and nothing else matters. You hurt people. But, that's life. The way it's supposed to be, I guess.

(silence)

It's hard, *hijo (son)*, it's hard. When you lose a child. The pain is so deep, your heart, your soul aches and there is nothing you can do about it.

EMILIANO. But, my mom…she's mad at the world…

ESPERANZA. Of course she is. Look at you, dead before you even really lived. *Es una tristeza, ¡una pinche tristeza! Tan guapo que estabas… (It's a shame, a fucking shame! You were so handsome…)* Look at you. A little toy soldier in your uniform that the *gobierno (government)* sent to fight their stupid war! *¿Qué ibas a saber tú de guerra? (What could you know about war?)* What could you know about hate and killing other human beings? *¿Qué? (What?)* You went over there full of fear, hoping that you would survive. But, hoping and praying isn't enough is it, *¿hijo?* You have to become someone… omething that you don't want to be. You have to become heartless and cold and ugly inside. Hateful and…

EMILIANO. I couldn't do it, *Nana.*

ESPERANZA. I know you couldn't, I know you couldn't.

(Silence. She goes to her night table where the tequila bottle sits.)

¿Quieres un tequilita, hijo? A little *copita?* One for the road, *como dicen. (Do you want a little tequila, son? A little shot. One for the road, as they say.)*

EMILIANO. Sure.

ESPERANZA. Shh… Don't tell your mom.

EMILIANO. How would I?

(She pours. They hold up their glasses.)

ESPERANZA. Here's to you, my *bis. (great grandson)* To your short but happy… Was it happy, *hijo?*

EMILIANO. Yes, I think it was.

ESPERANZA. To your short and happy life. *Salud, mi muertito. (Cheers, my little dead one.)* What do you want to drink to?

EMILIANO. To my short and happy life. To all the girls I left behind. To all the kisses and caresses and the lovemaking that was never to be. To the wedding I never had. To all the children and grandchildren I never had and to all the parties that I will miss; baptisms, holy communions, graduations; to all my birthdays that will never be; to all the sins I never committed and to all the promises I never kept; to the people I hurt, to the people I…killed. *(pause)* To life. It was short and sweet and the hard part is that it goes on, doesn't it, *Nana?*

ESPERANZA. Yes, it does, *hijo.* And one day your mother will get used to the pain of losing you and she will smile again, love again, live again.

EMILIANO. That's good.

(They clink.)

EMILIANO/ESPERANZA. *Salud.*

(They drink.)

Scene Five

(**GINA** *and* **VALENTINA** *continue reciting the rosary at the table:*)

VALENTINA. *(reading her laptop)* "Who was conceived by the Holy Spirit, born of the Virgin Mary, suffered under Pontius Pilate, was crucified, died, and was buried. He descended into hell…" What?

GINA. Really? Huh, I don't remember that.

(The doorbell rings. **VALENTINA** *runs to open it.)*

VALENTINA. Dad forgot his key again!

(She opens the door.)

OFFSTAGE VOICE. *Perdón. ¿Aquí es la casa de Elena García? (Pardon me. Is the the home of Elena Garcia?)*

*(*VALENTINA *looks at* GINA. *Tries to answer in her limited Spanish.)*

VALENTINA. *Sí, pero… (Yes, but…)* That's my Grandma. She's dead. She's been dead… *muerta for diez años. (dead for ten years)* Ten years.

*(*GINA *goes to the door.)*

GINA. *Yo soy su hija. ¿Qué se le ofrece? (I'm her daughter. How can I help you?)*

VOICE. *Soy nieto de un primo de ella. Acabo de llegar… (I'm the grandson of one of her cousins. I've just arrived…)*

GINA. *Pásale, pásale… (Come in, come in…)*

(A young man, **JUAN FRANCISCO**, *20s, enters. He is handsome and well mannered.)*

(Sound cue: church bells)

(The Litany of the Saints at Pope John Paul II's funeral is heard as **JUAN FRANCISCO** *enters.)*

Scene Six

(**SILVESTRE** *appears to* **ESPERANZA** *in her room.*)

ESPERANZA. *¿Silvestre? ¿Qué quieres?...* What do you want? What are you doing here? Did you come to confess me, or what?

SILVESTRE. You know why I'm here.

ESPERANZA. Yes, I know. To fuck up my life!

SILVESTRE. Don't talk like that, woman. How many times do I have to tell you...

ESPERANZA. Here comes the sermon.

(*She calls out.*) *¡Gina! ¡Gina!*

(*She becomes agitated.*)

You acted so saintly! But, you left and left me alone with our daughters.

SILVESTRE. There you go again! I didn't come to talk about that...

ESPERANZA. Of course, it's not convenient.

(*She calls out again.*) *¡Guillermina!*

SILVESTRE. You know why I'm here... I've come for you... Enough, Esperanza, I'm tired...

ESPERANZA. Of what?

SILVESTRE. Of waiting for you, woman. You should be considerate...

ESPERANZA. Considerate of whom? You?

SILVESTRE. Of everyone!

(**GINA** *enters and sees the* **ESPERANZA** *talking to herself.*)

ESPERANZA. *¡Vete mucho a la chingada! (Go fuck yourself!)*

Scene Seven

(**GINA** *enters* **ESPERANZA**'s *room.*

GINA. Shhh… *Nana,* you have company.

(**ESPERANZA** *looks at* **SILVESTRE**.)

ESPERANZA. *(re:* **SILVESTRE***) ¿Qué?* You can see him?

(**GINA** *ignores the question.*)

GINA. *(re:* **JUAN FRANCISCO**) He's a young man. He says he's related to you.

ESPERANZA. Really? How?

GINA. He says he's the great grandson of an old aunt.

ESPERANZA. *¿Cómo se llama? (What is his name?)*

GINA. Juan.

ESPERANZA. *¡Ya llegó San Juan Bautista! (John the Baptist is here!)*

GINA. No, his last name is not Bautista. His last name is Banda. Juan Francisco Banda.

ESPERANZA. Banda? Oh, then he is related. What does he look like? Is he tall?

GINA. Yes.

ESPERANZA. Like my grandfather. *¿Y guapo? (And handsome?)*

GINA. Yes.

ESPERANZA. *¿Inteligente? (Intelligent?)*

GINA. I don't know… We barely exchanged a few words before you started yelling.

ESPERANZA. Did you tell him that I'm crazy?

GINA. Yes.

ESPERANZA. Good! If I don't scream you don't come. I need papers for my cigarettes, *hija. (daughter)*

(**GINA** *takes rolling papers out of her pocket and hands them to her.*)

GINA. You know, if I didn't love you so much I would make you smoke outside. My house smells like cigarettes. It's embarrassing. It's bad enough I have to go to the store and ask for Zig Zags.

(**ESPERANZA** *takes the papers.*)

ESPERANZA. You don't love me. You used to love me. Now, I'm just a pain in the ass, *como dicen ustedes. (like you say)*

(**GINA** *feels bad.*)

GINA. That's not true, *Nana.* I love you.

ESPERANZA. If you loved me, you wouldn't be embarrassed...

GINA. ...of the cigarette smell, I said, not of you!

ESPERANZA. Then why haven't you brought my nephew up to meet me?

GINA. Because you won't take a bath.

ESPERANZA. See, you are embarrassed!

GINA. We're used to the *peste, (stench,) Nana,* but it might be too much for him to handle. He might faint.

ESPERANZA. *¡Ah, no seas tan exagerada! (Don't exaggerate!)* Put some perfume on me.

GINA. No, it will just make it worse.

ESPERANZA. Okay, then! *¡Chantajera! (Blackmailer!)* Tell Valentina to fill up the *tina* and I'll put on my pretty dress.

GINA. *¡Coqueta! (Flirt!)* Only for a man, *¿verdad? (right?)*

ESPERANZA. *Pues, sí. (Well, yes.)*

(**GINA** *begins to exit.*)

Gina, I have to tell you something, *m'ija... (my daughter)*

(**GINA** *stops and looks at* **ESPERANZA.**)

Bah... *Se me fue el patín... (I had a brain fart...)*

(**GINA** *exits. Music.*)

Scene Eight

(JUAN FRANCISCO *is sitting alone at the table when*
GINA's *husband,* RUDY, *50s, enters. He wears a suit
and tie and carries a briefcase.* JUAN FRANCISCO
quickly stands and extends his hand.)

JUAN FRANCISCO. *Buenas tardes. Perdón, me llamo Juan
Francisco. (Good afternoon. Pardon me, my name is Juan
Francisco.)*

(RUDY *is caught off guard, shakes hands.*)

RUDY. *Mucho gusto. (A pleasure.)*

(VALENTINA *enters from the kitchen with a glass of milk
and a bowl of cereal for* JUAN FRANCISCO.)

VALENTINA. Hi, Dad. (*She kisses* RUDY *on the cheek.*) Did you
meet Juan Francisco?

RUDY. Yes.

VALENTINA. He's related to Mom…somehow.

(JUAN FRANCISCO *nods, still standing.*)

Aquí está tu… (Here's your…) milk and your cereal.

JUAN FRANCISCO. *Gracias.*

(*He looks at them not knowing what to do.*)

VALENTINA. Go ahead. Eat.

RUDY. *Sí, sí, siga. (Yes, please continue.)*

(RUDY *goes to put his things down.* RUDY *gives*
VALENTINA *a "What's going on?" look.* VALENTINA
shrugs.)

VALENTINA. He just showed up at the door and said he was
related to *Nana* and so Mom let him in and he looked
really hungry. I mean, what could she do? (*pause*) Are
you mad?

RUDY. Why would I be mad?

VALENTINA. I don't know. I can never tell how you guys will
react to things these days. If you ask me, I think it's
kind of rude to just show up with no notice, don't you?

RUDY. Yeah, but, that's the way Mexicans from Mexico are. They just show up.

(JUAN FRANCISCO *stops eating and stands.*)

JUAN FRANCISCO. *(with heavy accent)* I think you should know that I understand English. And I am very sorry that I just came here without letting you know. I know it is rude. But, well, I apologize.

(RUDY *and* VALENTINA, *embarrassed.*)

RUDY. Oh, sorry, man. We're sorry, too. We shouldn't be talking about people like that...

(*He looks at* VALENTINA. *The three of them look at each other for a sec.*)

VALENTINA. Awkward...

(*They laugh.*)

RUDY. Sit down. Sit down, man. Finish your meal.

(ESPERANZA *from offstage.*)

ESPERANZA. *(offstage)* ¡Valentina!

(VALENTINA *begins to exit.*)

VALENTINA. Be right back. *(to* RUDY*)* Busted.

(RUDY *and* JUAN FRANCISCO *are left alone, not knowing what to say to each other.*)

RUDY. Excuse me.

(*He exits.* JUAN FRANCISCO *is left alone and continues to eat.*)

(*Footage of coverage of Pope John Paul II's funeral continues.*)

(RUDY *enters without his tie and jacket on, carrying a beer.* JUAN FRANCISCO *stands up again.*)

Can I get you a beer?

JUAN FRANCISCO. No, I do not drink.

RUDY. Oh, okay.

JUAN FRANCISCO. But, can I have more milk?

(**RUDY** *looks surprised.*)

RUDY. Oh… Sure.

(**JUAN FRANCISCO** *hands him his glass and smiles.*)

JUAN FRANCISCO. Thank you.

(**RUDY** *goes to get the milk.* **JUAN FRANCISCO** *sits down
again.* **GINA** *enters and* **JUAN FRANCISCO** *stands up.*)

¿Cómo está mi tía? (How is my aunt?)

GINA. *Muy bien. Se está bañando. No te quiere recibir sin
arreglarse. (She's well. She's taking a bath. She didn't want to
see you without getting dressed up.)*

JUAN FRANCISCO. *Ay, que no se preocupe. (Oh, she shouldn't
have bothered.)*

GINA. *Ya sabes cómo son… (You know how they are…)*

(**RUDY** *enters with a glass of milk.*)

I didn't know you were home… Did you meet…

RUDY. Yes.

(*He puts the glass of milk on the table.*)

JUAN FRANCISCO. Thank you…*tío. (uncle)*

(**RUDY** *is surprised.*)

RUDY. No, problem.

(**RUDY** *kisses* **GINA.**)

GINA. *Juan Francisco es nieto de un sobrino de Nana. (Juan
Francisco is the grandson of one of Nana's nephews.)*

(*to* **JUAN FRANCISCO**) *¿Verdad? (Right?)*

RUDY. He speaks English, Gina.

GINA. You do, Juan Francisco?

JUAN FRANCISCO. Yes, I do, *tía. (aunt)* And my name is too
long. You should call me Johnny or Frankie? Which
one do you think?

GINA. Johnny.

RUDY. Frankie.

GINA. Frankie.

RUDY. Johnny.

JUAN FRANCISCO. I know it is so hard to decide, *¿verdad?* *(right?)* But, I think Frankie is better, don't you? Like Frankie Valli or Frank Zappa.

GINA. Okay.

RUDY. Yeah, sure… Frankie.

(They look at each other not sure about their new guest.)

Scene Nine

(**ESPERANZA** *is sitting on the bed while* **VALENTINA** *tries to untangle her long, white hair.*)

ESPERANZA. Not so hard! *¡Me duele! (It hurts!)*

VALENTINA. It's all tangled, that's why! If you washed it more often...

ESPERANZA. *Ay, ustedes. (Oh, you people.)* You're so obsessed with bathing. When I was little I used to take a bath once a week... in the river.

VALENTINA. If I had to take a bath in a river I would only bathe once a week, too.

ESPERANZA. Even after we had a bathtub, we only took a bath once a week.

VALENTINA. That's gross, *Nana.*

ESPERANZA. Taking a bath every day is unnatural. *La cáscara guarda al palo. (The bark protects the stem.)*

VALENTINA. What?

ESPERANZA. It's bad for your skin. Why do you think I look so good for my age?

VALENTINA. Because you're still alive?

(**ESPERANZA** *smacks* **VALENTINA.**)

Ow!

ESPERANZA. *¡Malcriada! (Ill-bred!)* Just because I'm old doesn't mean I can't kick your ass, *como dicen ustedes. (like you say)*

(**VALENTINA** *laughs.*)

VALENTINA. Why don't you cut your hair, *Nana?* That way we won't have to go through this every time you take a bath – once a month. Don't you know women of a certain age should not have long hair?

ESPERANZA. Who told you that? Old women are like babies. If we cut our hair, no one can tell if we are a man or a woman.

(**VALENTINA** *laughs.* **ESPERANZA** *smiles.*)

I like to hear you laugh, *hija. (daughter)* Even if it is at my expense… Laugh, laugh!

(She sings.)

AYYY QUE DARLE GUSTO AL GUSTO, LA VIDA PRONTO SE ACABA…

(Oh, let's give delight, delight, life is over quickly…)

Life is over before you know it.

VALENTINA. *(sarcastically)* Oh, really?

*(***VALENTINA*** *puts down the brush and* **ESPERANZA** *touches her hand.)*

ESPERANZA. Look at your hands, *hija, (daughter)* they look just like mine when I was young. My *abuelita (grandmother)* would say *Como te ves me vi, como me ves te verás.* "The way you look, I looked. The way I look, you will look." Loose translation.

VALENTINA. You had a *Nana?*

ESPERANZA. *Claro. (Of course.)* Your great, great… great grandmother. A little *india. (Indian)* She taught me many things. She blessed me with *la palabra antigua. (ancient word)* The words of the elders. They were written thousands of years ago by our *progenitores (ancestors)* and they were passed down to me and I am supposed to pass them down to all of you… But, now, I can't remember… I can't remember…

Scene Ten

(**RUDY** *and* **FRANKIE** *continue watching the coverage of Pope John Paul II's funeral on TV.*)

FRANKIE. Where is the Bradbury building?

RUDY. What?

FRANKIE. The Bradbury building where they made the movie Bladerunner.

RUDY. Oh, it's downtown. On Broadway, I think.

FRANKIE. I was telling Valentina that I would really like to see that building. I was telling Valentina that I have dreamed about seeing that building. That and The Dakota, where they shot John Lennon. But, that is in New York. And of course, the Statue of Liberty, but that is in New York, too.

RUDY. Right.

FRANKIE. I would like to see the Capitol Records Tower.

RUDY. How long are you planning on staying?

(**JUAN FRANCISCO** *looks at him.*)

In L.A., I mean.

FRANKIE. In L.A.? I don't know. If I find work. If I fall in love with a blonde, beautiful girl…

RUDY. Where do you think you will find a blonde beautiful girl to fall in love with?

FRANKIE. I don't know. Maybe at the Capitol Records Tower!

(**RUDY** *laughs.*)

Or at the Grauman's Chinese Theater!

(**VALENTINA** *enters.*)

VALENTINA. Juanfra. Come up and say hi to *Nana*.

(**JUAN FRANCISCO** *jumps up.*)

JUAN FRANCISCO. Finally!

(**VALENTINA** *leads him up the stairs as* **GINA** *comes down. She goes to* **RUDY**.)

GINA. How long is he planning on staying?

RUDY. I don't know.

GINA. Does he have a place to stay?

RUDY. You mean, you don't know?

GINA. I didn't ask him.

RUDY. I didn't either. He's a nice kid…

GINA. But, I don't want him here.

RUDY. What if he doesn't have a place…

GINA. I don't want him here!

RUDY. Okay. *(pause)* Don't get upset. If you don't want him to stay… It's fine. I understand. But, he's your relative, you tell him.

(**GINA** *gives* **RUDY** *a look.*)

Scene Eleven

(ESPERANZA's *room is lit with dim lights and candles.*
We see her in silhouette as VALENTINA *enters with* JUAN
FRANCISCO *walking cautiously behind her.*)

ESPERANZA. *Pásale. No tengas miedo. No te voy a morder. (Come*
in. Don't be afraid. I won't bite you.)

(VALENTINA *pushes* JUAN FRANCISCO *toward the*
ESPERANZA.

VALENTINA. Juanfra, go on.

(JUAN FRANCISCO *moves close to the* ESPERANZA.)

FRANKIE. *Hola, tía. (Hello, Aunt.) (He over-enunciates.) Me*
llamo Juan Francisco. Soy bisnieto de su primo Enrique
Banda. (My name is Juan Francisco. I'm the great grandson
of your cousin Enrique Banda.)

(*He takes her hand and kisses her cheek.*)

ESPERANZA. *Hola, hijo. (Hello, son.)*

(VALENTINA *laughs.*)

VALENTINA. She can hear and understand perfectly well.
He speaks English, *Nana.*

ESPERANZA. But, he speaks Spanish, too. And if there is one
thing I hate is two people who speak Spanish speaking
to each other in English! I only talk to you and your
mother and father in English because you can barely
speak Spanish. You are *pochos! ¡Pochos! (Not Mexicans!)*

(*She changes her tone.*)

Pero este niño no es pocho. Este es mexicano. De México,
¿verdad hijo? (But, this young boy is not a pocho. He is
Mexican, from México, right, son?)

JUAN FRANCISCO. *¡Del mero, mero! (Yes, from right there!)*

ESPERANZA. *¡Así me gusta! ¿Quieres un tequilita, hijo? ¿Una*
copita de bienvenida? (That's what I like to hear! Do you
want a little tequila, son? A little shot to welcome you?)

JUAN FRANCISCO. *No, gracias, tía. No tomo. (No, thank you, Aunt. I don't drink.)*

(ESPERANZA is disappointed.)

ESPERANZA. *¿Qué? ¡No seas menso! Valentina, sírvenos unos tequilas. (What? Don't be silly. Valentina, serve us some tequila.)*

(VALENTINA pours the shots.)

VALENTINA. *Nana,* are you going to force Juanfra to drink?

ESPERANZA. *¿Juanfra? ¿Por qué le dices Juanfra? Su nombre es Juan Francisco.(Why do you call him Juanfra? His name is Juan Francisco.)*

VALENTINA. He wants us to call him Frankie.

(ESPERANZA glares at Juan Francisco.)

ESPERANZA. *¿Qué, estás pendejo? (Are you stupid?)*

JUAN FRANCISCO. *¿Perdón? (Pardon?)*

ESPERANZA. *¡Te llamas Juan Francisco como mi abuelo! ¡Salud! (Your name is Juan Francisco, like by grandfather! Cheers!)*

(JUAN FRANCISCO drinks the entire shot. He gasps for air. ESPERANZA rolls her eyes.)

Ay, hijo, ¡qué verde estás! (Oh, son, you are so green!)

(JUAN FRANCISCO recovers.)

VALENTINA. Ah, *Nana* called you green!

JUAN FRANCISCO. I have never drank tequila before.

ESPERANZA. What a strange Mexican you are.

(JUAN FRANCISCO grimaces at the burn in his chest.)

It's good for you, *hombre!* Valentina, turn on the lamp so that I can get a better look at my nephew.

(VALENTINA turns on the lamp to reveal that ESPERANZA is wearing a pretty, flowered, cotton moo moo dress, her hair is combed with a flower in it and she has on make up that is a few shades too light and bright red lipstick. She looks pretty for a woman of her age.)

(ESPERANZA looks at JUAN FRANCISCO.)

ESPERANZA. *(cont.) Mira nomás. Qué chulo estás. (Look at that. You are gorgeous.)* You look like my brother, Martin...

(She touches his face.)

He fought with Emiliano Zapata and he was with him the day he died, the day they betrayed him...

JUAN FRANCISCO. Yes?

ESPERANZA. You know why people revere Zapata more than they do Pancho Villa?

JUAN FRANCISCO. Of course. Because he fought for the land and for the indigenous people. He spoke *Náhuatl*...

ESPERANZA. Yes, yes, and what else?

JUAN FRANCISCO. Because he said, "It is better to die on your feet than to live on your knees."

ESPERANZA. *¿Y? (And?)*

JUAN FRANCISCO. Because he said *Tierra y Libertad! (Land and Liberty!)*

ESPERANZA. No! That is not why!

VALENTINA. Why then?

ESPERANZA. *¡Porque estaba bien chulo, el cabrón! (He was handsome, that's why!)* Those dark piercing eyes, the mustache, *su traje de charro...* (his *charro** suit) And yes, his passion for liberty and justice made him absolutely irresistible.

(They all sit on that thought for a second.)

How long are you staying?

VALENTINA. He doesn't know yet.

ESPERANZA. She always answers for people when she shouldn't. Tell me, how long are you staying?

JUAN FRANCISCO. I don't know yet.

VALENTINA. I told you.

(She ignores **VALENTINA.** *)*

---

*A traditional Mexican horseman/horsewoman.

ESPERANZA. How can you not know? What are your plans? What are you dreams?

VALENTINA. He wants to see the Capitol Records Building.

ESPERANZA. The what?

JUAN FRANCISCO. Well, I have been wanting to come here for a long time, *tía. (aunt)*

ESPERANZA. But, why?

JUAN FRANCISCO. Why?

ESPERANZA. Yes, everybody has a reason for coming. Some of us come out of necessity and desperation. Some of us come on a whim. And...

VALENTINA. And some of you come because you want to see the Bradbury Building where they shot the movie Bladerunner.

(**ESPERANZA** *glares at* **VALENTINA.**)

ESPERANZA. If we ignore her she might go away. *A ver, dime. (Go on, tell me.)*

JUAN FRANCISCO. It's because it is the best country in the world, *tía. (aunt)*

ESPERANZA. Uh huh... And what makes you say that?

JUAN FRANCISCO. Everybody knows it, *tía.* As soon as I crossed the border I could see that everything was in order, not like in *México* where everything is out of order and ever since I was little I would hear people talk about somebody coming here and becoming successful and rich and there is opportunity here, *tía.* Over there, what is there for me? Life is not fair, *tía.* My mother, she works and works to provide for me and my little brfive hundred *pesos.* five hundred *pesos, tía.* That is what I can make here in one day even if I just wash dishes. I want to work and study and send money to my mother and help her and once I am successful here I will send for her and my brother and we will have a good life here, *tía.*

VALENTINA. And he wants to fall in love with a beautiful blonde!

JUAN FRANCISCO. Well, she doesn't have to be blonde. She can have red hair or brown hair...

VALENTINA. He's going to meet her at the Grauman's Chinese Theater.

ESPERANZA. Isn't your mother calling you?

VALENTINA. No!

ESPERANZA. How did you get here? Did a coyote cross you?

JUAN FRANCISCO. No, *tía*, I have a visa. Not for working, but... I have finished school. But, there is nothing for me in *México*. The best job in *México* is to be a *narcotraficante (drug smuggler)* and I cannot do that.

ESPERANZA. No, *hijo*, that's worse than going to war...

JUAN FRANCISCO. I know. Everyday there is a dead body in the street, sometimes with the head cut off. Friends I grew up with have become murderers and I am always afraid there. I understand, though... They chose it because there is nothing else. I chose to come here.

*(He hands her his glass for more tequila. **ESPERANZA** smirks.)*

ESPERANZA. *¿No que no? (Didn't you say no?)*

JUAN FRANCISCO. It feels good, *tía*. I feel good here with you, with my family. I have hope.

(silence)

ESPERANZA. *Qué bueno, hijo. Qué bueno. (That's good, son. That's good.)*

(She drags on her cigarette and blows out the smoke as an old memory comes over her. She begins to sing, "Cancion Mixteca" by José López Alavez.*)

*(**VALENTINA** begins to laugh.)*

No le hagas caso. (Don't pay attention to her.) She knows nothing about being a Mexican.

VALENTINA. Yes, I do.

ESPERANZA. No, you don't. If you did, you would know that when a relative arrives you greet them, feed them, give

---

*Please see Music Use Note on page 3

them a *tequilita (little tequila)* and then you sing songs that make them remember…

QUE LEJOS ESTOY DEL SUELO

DONDE HE NACIDO.

INMENSA NOSTALGIA INVADE MI PENSAMIENTO…

(How far I am from the ground
Where I was born.
An immense nostalgia invades my thoughts…)

JUAN FRANCISCO. *No, tía, me vas a ser llorar…* *(No, Aunt, you're going to make me cry…)*

(She hands him her handkerchief.)

ESPERANZA. *(to* **VALENTINA***) Ya ves. (You see.)* I've been telling you to learn that song.

(to **JUAN FRANCISCO***)* She has a beautiful voice, just like her mother. But, she doesn't think I know anything.

VALENTINA. Yes, I do.

JUAN FRANCISCO. My *tía* Gina sings?

VALENTINA. She used to…

ESPERANZA. Not anymore. *Se le acabó el ánimo… (Her spirit is gone…)*

(to **VALENTINA***)* Where is he going to sleep?

*(***VALENTINA** *shrugs.)*

VALENTINA. I don't know.

Scene Twelve

(**GINA** *sits on the couch and continues to watch the coverage of the Pope's funeral.* **RUDY** *enters from backstage with a drink in his hand. He may have had one too many.*)

RUDY. The thing about the Pope is that he was so right about some things and so wrong about others, you know?

GINA. He was a good Pope... considering.

RUDY. What do you mean? He's the head of the Catholic Church!

GINA. Okay, maybe I don't hate the Catholic Church like you do.

RUDY. I don't hate the Catholic Church. Sometimes, I like the Catholic Church.

GINA. Sometimes?

RUDY. Yeah, like when it defends the undocumented and preaches compassion for the poor...when it's against the war and the death penalty. But...

GINA. Here we go...

RUDY. You know what, Gina, I was a good Catholic! I went to Catholic school, I made all my sacraments, I served mass as an altar boy in Vietnam...

GINA. ...and that's why you didn't see any action...

RUDY. And I appreciate that. But, we can't ignore the contradictions.

GINA. I'm not...

RUDY. Like it's a contradiction to condemn homosexuality when half of the priests in the world are gay!

GINA. Half?

RUDY. Okay, two-thirds.

GINA. Where did you get those choice statistics, from my brother Bobby? He thinks everybody's gay, including you.

RUDY. And the way the Church handled the pedophile priests, Gina, come on… And guess who's paying off that settlement? The Latino community.

(**GINA** *gives him a look.*)

That's right because we give to this archdiocese. We are this archdiocese! All those dollars on all those Sundays in all those churches add up!

(**GINA** *sighs.*)

GINA. Okay, I liked the Pope. So, I'm wrong and you're right. Are you happy?

RUDY. No, I want you to argue a little. You're taking all the fun out of this.

GINA. I'm not up for fun these days, Rudy.

(*She stands and crosses to the table where* **EMILIANO**'*s photo stands.*)

(*Silence. Two lost souls sharing a pain that only they can feel.*)

I had a dream about him. He was so happy. He was saying, "Mom it's so beautiful here, I love it." And I was upset because I didn't think he missed me. It was like I was jealous of heaven…

RUDY. No one was ever good enough for him in your eyes…not even heaven.

GINA. Don't tease. I woke up and I was angry.

RUDY. Hello?

GINA. No, because I wanted to feel him close to me…and I don't. *(silence)* Do you… I mean, do you think he's up there somewhere? Do you believe…

RUDY. I don't know… I used to. When I was a kid I believed that if I was good I'd go to heaven…where there would be clouds and angels and… God. But, now… I don't know…

GINA. When did we stop believing? When we were young and we lost the baby, we believed. Why didn't we teach our kids to believe in anything? The thought of never seeing him again… I can't…

RUDY. Gina, come on...

GINA. How can you just...

RUDY. What can we do, Gina? What can we do? I open my
eyes in the morning and I miss him. I brush my teeth
and I miss him, I eat breakfast and I miss him. I drive
to work and I miss him and that's the way it goes...
And we can tear ourselves apart by placing blame and
questioning ourselves and what if we would have done
this or that or why didn't we do this or that and what
good will it do, Gina? What? He's gone.

(He holds back tears.)

He's gone...

(He picks up the large envelope on the table.)

Are we going to open it?

GINA. Not now. I don't want to know. It doesn't matter
anyway.

*(**GINA** exits.)*

Scene Thirteen

(A knock and the door opens and **GINA**'s *younger brother,* **BOBBY**, *now in his 40s, enters stage left. He is wearing tight pants, a tight top, his hair is over treated and kind of spiked up in a mess. He looks like he partied a little too much the night before.)*

BOBBY. Hello? It's me.

*(***BOBBY*** sees ***JUAN FRANCISCO*** and stops in his tracks.)*

JUAN FRANCISCO. Hello, my name is Juan Francisco, but you can call me Frankie.

*(***JUAN FRANCISCO*** offers his hand and ***BOBBY*** takes it.)*

BOBBY. Nice to meet you.

JUAN FRANCISCO. *Mucho gusto. (A pleasure.)* I am Gina's nephew. From *México.*

BOBBY. Really? I would have never guessed it.

*(***BOBBY*** crosses to ***VALENTINA*** at the table and gives her a kiss on the cheek.)*

VALENTINA. Hi, Nino. This is Juanfra?

JUAN FRANCISCO. Frankie...

VALENTINA. This is my mom's brother, Bobby. Your uncle too, I guess...

BOBBY. Cousin...

VALENTINA. No, because if...

(He interrupts her.)

BOBBY. Where's your mom?

VALENTINA. She's around.

BOBBY. Is your Auntie Betty here yet?

VALENTINA. Uh uh. Is she supposed to be?

BOBBY. We're going shopping and taking your mom with us.

VALENTINA. Can I go?

BOBBY. I guess…

VALENTINA. My Mom's obsessed with the Pope's funeral.

BOBBY. Poor Pope. He was so cute.

VALENTINA. He was against gays, you know.

BOBBY. Well, nobody's perfect. I wonder who they'll pick to replace him.

VALENTINA. Who cares?

BOBBY. Shush. You're gonna go to hell, you know that? *(pause)* Then, I'll never be rid of you.

(He laughs at his own joke! GINA enters.)

GINA. What's so funny?

BOBBY. Nothing's funny. Your daughter is a heretic, that's all. And why didn't you tell me you had a relative visiting from the motherland?

VALENTINA. From the motherland?

BOBBY. Yes, the motherland, smarty pants. Meaning, Mexico. Gina, when was the last time you spanked her? Get the belt.

VALENTINA. My parents don't believe in spanking…

BOBBY. And look what happened…

JUAN FRANCISCO. ¿De veras? *(Really?)* My mother hit us all the time.

BOBBY. And look how polite he is…

(He turns to GINA and mouths He's gay.)

I can't believe she didn't spank you guys. She used to beat us with her shoe, pull our hair, yell at us..

VALENTINA. Really, Mom?

GINA. He's exaggerating…

(GINA's sister, BETTY, now in her 50s, enters. Tight pants, tight top, a big bag and over treated messy hair. She looks like she partied too much the night before.)

VALENTINA. Hi, Auntie Betty.

BETTY. Hi, m'ija. *(my daughter)* It's fucking hot out there!

(She sees JUAN FRANCISCO.)

Oh, sorry.

BOBBY. Excuse her manners, Frankie. She can't say two words without dropping the "F" bomb.

(**JUAN FRANCISCO** *stands.*)

GINA. Juan Francisco...

BOBBY. Frankie...

GINA. Frankie, this is my sister, Betty. She's your Aunt, too.

BETTY. *Hola... (Hello...)*

(*She looks at* **GINA**)

Frankie?

(*He offers his hand and she takes it.*)

Me llamo Beatriz, (My name is Beatriz,) but you can call me Betty.

JUAN FRANCISCO. *Mucho gusto, Betty. (A pleasure, Betty.)* (*to* **BOBBY**) What is the "F" bomb?

(**VALENTINA** *laughs.*)

ESPERANZA. *(offstage) ¡Beatriz!*

(**BETTY** *looks up.*)

BETTY. How does she know I'm here? *(She calls up.) Allí voy, Nana! (There I go, Nana.)* (*to* **BOBBY**) I'll be right back. Just gonna say hi. Wanna come?

BOBBY. No, I'll wait here. The last time I went up there, I was there for five hours and got drunk. Hurry, though. Don't get too into the *chisme. (gossip)*

(**JUAN FRANCISCO** *looks at* **VALENTINA**.)

VALENTINA. Auntie Betty tells her all about her love life and my *Nana* eats it up.

GINA. Yeah, they have a great relationship. She doesn't have to take care of her.

(*She is sorry as soon as she says it. She knows she sounds bitter.*)

I mean, I'm not complaining or anything..

BOBBY. No, of course not.

(**GINA** *exits upstage right with* **VALENTINA** *not far behind.*)

(**JUAN FRANCISCO** *looks at* **BOBBY**.)

JUAN FRANCISCO. You are gay, right?

Scene Fourteen

(ESPERANZA *and* BETTY *are upstairs smoking and talking.* BETTY *is in the middle of a story.*)

BETTY. And as we sat there in the restaurant looking into each other's eyes, the soft glow of the candlelight on his face, suddenly a beautiful lady appeared with three little children right beside her...

ESPERANZA. An apparition?

BETTY. No, his wife and kids!

ESPERANZA. *¡Desgraciado! (Ingrate!)*

BETTY. It's a shame, though. He seemed so perfect.

ESPERANZA. The married ones always do.

BETTY. He was so kind, romantic, considerate...

ESPERANZA. That should have tipped you off.

(BETTY *sighs.*)

BETTY. Yeah, you're right. I don't know *Nana*, maybe I'm destined never to meet the right, man.

ESPERANZA. No one is destined for anything. You create your own destiny. You haven't found *el bueno. (the good one)*

BETTY. Good men are hard to find. They're either married, divorced with kids, widowed or too old to be any fun in bed or just plain ass holes.

ESPERANZA. *Ay, mi hija, (Oh, my daughter,)* I gave up trying to figure out men in the '20s.

BETTY. In your twenties?

ESPERANZA. No, in the '20s. You know 1920, 1925...

BETTY. *Nana*, that's almost a hundred years ago.

ESPERANZA. How many times have you been married?

BETTY. *(sighs)* Four...

(ESPERANZA *tries to remember.*)

ESPERANZA. *A ver... the gringito ese (Let's see... the little gringo)* with the red hair that looked like...

BETTY. John F. Kennedy...

ESPERANZA. ...and then *el Cubano ese.* *(that Cuban)* The one that looked like...

BETTY. ...Fidel Castro.

ESPERANZA. And then the one who looked like your father, Carlos...

BETTY. ...and acted like him, too.

ESPERANZA. And who was the fourth one?

BETTY. The *Mexicano,* remember? The one I married to help him get his papers.

ESPERANZA. *Ah sí. ¿Y te pagó? (Oh, yes. Did he pay you?)*

BETTY. No, I didn't have the heart to take his money...

ESPERANZA. Then why did you marry him?

BETTY. Because I loved him...

ESPERANZA. *¿Y qué pasó? (And what happened?)*

BETTY. He came out as soon as he got his green card.

ESPERANZA. *¡Pa' acabarla de fregar! (That's all you needed!)*

BETTY. I know...

ESPERANZA. *Ay, hija, eres demasiada buena. Los hombres son hijos de la mala vida. (Oh, my daughter, you are too nice. Men love to be treated badly.)* You have to treat them mean. Listen to the voice of experience. The worse you treat them, the more they want you.

BETTY. I know, I'm too nice.

ESPERANZA. *¡Pero te pasas! (Way too nice!)*

BETTY. But, I don't like being mean. It makes me feel bad. I feel fake. You know we can't lie.

ESPERANZA. There's a difference between pretending and lying.

(**BETTY** *smiles.*)

BETTY. Okay, we'll see. I don't know, *Nana*... Don't you think that sometimes, what's meant to be is meant to be? It's not like I didn't meet nice guys who loved me... I just didn't love them...

ESPERANZA. What's meant to be is what you make it to be. *Tú también eres hija de la mala vida. (You like to be treated badly, too.)* You like the ones that treat you bad and don't like the ones who treat you good.

(**BETTY** *drags on the cigarette.*)

BETTY. My therapist says I have "daddy issues."

ESPERANZA. *Ay, sí, hija.* Your father was a *cabrón. (asshole)*

BETTY. My JFK fascination... And my depression when he died... My therapist says all that was because of my daddy issues.

ESPERANZA. *¿Que 'ta loca? (Is she crazy?)* The whole world was depressed when President Kennedy died.

(She remembers.) Yo sabía que lo iban a matar por católico. (I knew they were going to kill him because he was Catholic.)

(sighs) Tan chulo que estaba... (He was so gorgeous.)

No, *hija.* Don't be paying people to tell you what's wrong with you. If you are going to pay someone, pay them to tell you how good you are, how pretty you are, how sexy you are. That will make you feel better. But, to tell you, you have issues? Who needs that?

(**BETTY** *laughs.*)

BETTY. *Nana,* you always make me feel better!

ESPERANZA. And I don't charge.

(**BETTY** *laughs.* **BOBBY** *calls from downstairs.*)

BOBBY. *(offstage)* Betty! Come on, we gotta go!

ESPERANZA. Is that Bobby? Why didn't he come up to say "Hi?"

(**BETTY** *kisses the* **ESPERANZA.**)

BETTY. We don't have time...

ESPERANZA. *Ay, qué cabroncito este. (That little shit.)*

BETTY. Gotta go, *Nana,* before Gina changes her mind. We're taking her shopping. She has to get out.

ESPERANZA. *Ándale pues. (Alright then.)* Tell Gina to buy me some lipstick.

(**BETTY** *exits.*)

And *tabaco* for my cigarettes! *(pause)* And *tequila!*

Scene Fifteen

(**BOBBY** *is gathering his things to leave.*)

BOBBY. Betty, Gina, come on!

(**GINA** *enters from one direction.* **BETTY** *enters from the other.*)

We got to go. I have to get back to the shop. I lost my assistant.

GINA. What happened?

BOBBY. Oh, she ran off with some man. Know anybody who wants a job working for an extremely generous, extremely sexy, extremely talented hair dresser?

(**VALENTINA** *begins to open her mouth, but he stops her with –*)

Shush!

JUAN FRANCISCO. I want a job!

BOBBY. Really?

VALENTINA. No, Juanfra, you don't want to…

JUAN FRANCISCO. Yes, I have to find work. If I don't find work soon, I think my *tía* will get tired of me and want me to go back to *México*…

BOBBY. I didn't know this was a long-term "visit." He's staying here?

VALENTINA. Yes.

(**GINA** *looks at* **VALENTINA.**)

Nana told him he could.

(**GINA** *doesn't know what to say.*)

JUAN FRANCISCO. If it's okay with you, *tía.*

GINA. Sure. You can sleep on the couch.

JUAN FRANCISCO. Thank you, *tía.*

(**BOBBY** *looks at* **JUAN FRANCISCO.**)

BOBBY. Do you have papers?

VALENTINA. No, he doesn't.

BOBBY. Perfect! Wanna come with?

JUAN FRANCISCO. Yes, if it is okay.

BOBBY. Of course, it's okay. Everybody has to experience the ally once in their life.

Scene Sixteen

(ESPERANZA *is praying when* SILVESTRE *appears again.*)

ESPERANZA. ¿*Otra vez?* (Again?)

SILVESTRE. *Y no me voy hasta...* (And I'm not leaving until...)

ESPERANZA. ¿*Hasta qué? ¿Hasta que me vaya contigo? ¡No hombre, nada que me voy!* (Until what? Until I go with you?) No, sir, I'm not going. Don't you see that I have to take care of our family? What will they do without me?

SILVESTRE. Rest...

ESPERANZA. *Ingrato.* (Ingrate.) Do you want me to abandon them the way you abandoned us?

SILVESTRE. I left because you wanted me to leave... Because you said you didn't love me... Because you...

ESPERANZA. ¡*Ay, sí, sí!*

(She cries.)

Ya, perdón. I'm sorry. Forgive me for making you lose your way. I thought that if we ran away together that everything would be different. That you would forget about your past. But, no, you were too faithful. You were too good. It's good to be good. But, you were way too good.

(She pours herself a shot of tequila. She looks at him.)

¿*Una copita?* (Want a shot?)

(He gives in.)

SILVESTRE. *'Ta bueno.* (Alright.)

(She pours him a glass. She smiles.)

I did love you, Esperanza.

(She looks at him.)

ESPERANZA. In your own way.

SILVESTRE. In my own way. The only way that I could.

ESPERANZA. It wasn't so bad, after all. We were happy for a long time.

SILVESTRE. With the girls, we had no choice.

ESPERANZA. You never gave your true love to me. You never gave me your being. Because you were never really mine. Isn't that right?

(He doesn't answer.)

Contéstame, pues. (Well, answer me.)

SILVESTRE. *Sí, es cierto. (Yes, it's true.)* I was never yours. But I am a man and you were so beautiful. You pulled me away. I could feel your gaze upon me when I was saying mass, when I put the host in your mouth, when I confessed you. You pulled me away and I couldn't resist…

(silence)

ESPERANZA. I always knew that your heart and soul belonged to…

SILVESTRE. …to God. To God and no one else.

*(**SILVESTRE** disappears.)*

ESPERANZA. *Lo sabía. (I knew it.)*

(She shakes her head in sorrow.)

How could I fall in love with a priest? How could I compete with God? *Que pinche suerte. (What shitty luck.)*

(Footage: Pope John Paul II is laid to rest)

Scene Seventeen

(**RUDY** *is alone watching T.V. He puts a shot glass and a bottle of tequila on the table. He looks at the envelope on the table. He pours himself a shot. He sits. He drinks. He reaches for the envelope. There is a knock at the door.* **RUDY** *goes to open it. It is* **JOHNNY**, *now in his 50', wearing a cap and an old army jacket, carrying a guitar.*)

RUDY. Hey, Johnny…

(**JOHNNY** *enters.*)

JOHNNY. Hey…

RUDY. You just missed Gina, Betty and Bobby.

JOHNNY. I know. I saw their cars and waited 'til they left. Not that I don't love them. I just don't want to hear their shit. You know what I'm saying?

RUDY. I hear you… How you doing? Good?

(*He shrugs.*)

JOHNNY. Still here. I guess that's good, no? Hey, can I borrow twenty bucks until next week?

RUDY. Sure.

(*He takes a twenty out of his wallet and hands it to* **JOHNNY**.)

JOHNNY. I'll pay you back when I get my disability, okay?

RUDY. Don't worry about it. You want a beer?

JOHNNY. No, but I'll have some of that tequila there.

(**RUDY** *heads for the kitchen.*)

They should be a while, right?

RUDY. (*offstage*) Should be.

(**RUDY** *enters with a glass as* **JOHNNY** *pulls a joint out of his pocket.*)

JOHNNY. You got Febreeze, right?

RUDY. Yeah, think so.

JOHNNY. That shit is good.

(He lights up and holds up the joint. He takes a drag and hands it to **RUDY.** *)*

…and so is this. Remember the first time we smoked grass?

RUDY. No.

JOHNNY. Neither do I…

(They smile.)

RUDY. It was in the Nam… The first time I smoked grass was in Vietnam.

JOHNNY. Yeah, me too, I guess. Vietnam, *'sta cabrón, ese… (it was fucked)* Remember?

RUDY. I try not to.

JOHNNY. Me too. *(silence)* I'm sorry I didn't make it to the funeral. I can't…do funerals. I can't do military funerals. The gun salutes, they…

RUDY. I understand.

JOHNNY. I think about Miliano. Rudy, he was so smart and he didn't have to go. He enlisted, just like you. Me? I was drafted and what we saw and what we had to do… It breaks my heart about Miliano… He had no business seeing that kind of shit. He was good and kind and…

(He stops before he begins to cry.)

I'm sorry… I'm sorry, man… I'm still all fucked up, you know that… You were lucky, Rudy.

You were smarter than I was.

RUDY. No, I wasn't.

JOHNNY. Don't say you weren't! You were, man! You were! You were smart and you maneuvered your way through the system without having to do… the things… Me, people like me. Stupid people like me, Rudy. Dumb kids who didn't know what we were in for and they sent us out there and we didn't know what hit us and the only way we could cope is to drink and smoke and shoot up and the kids now... It's the same now, Rudy, it's the same and for what? For what? I think about these kids over there in Iraq... All scared, all afraid... They're all afraid... pretending not to be... Us, at least we were "fighting communism." But, these kids... Another generation of fucked-uptedness... Because the damaged goods are gonna come home one day, Rudy, to join the rest of us. And we won't be ready for them, just like they weren't ready for us... *(silence)* Maybe that's why God took him, Rudy. To spare him the pain.

RUDY. I wish I could believe that.

*(Silence. **JOHNNY** tries to recuperate.)*

JOHNNY. How's my sister? How's Gina? Still mean?

*(**RUDY** gives him a look.)*

RUDY. Come on, Johnny.

JOHNNY. Just kidding.

RUDY. She's broken. She's existing. But, she's broken.

*(**RUDY** drags.)*

JOHNNY. You know, I think about our childhood sometimes and it's a wonder we're not more screwed up than we are. You know what I'm saying? I mean, none of us stayed married except Gina and that's because you're afraid of her.

RUDY. I'm not afraid of her.

JOHNNY. You're not?

RUDY. Yeah, I guess I am. I mean, not afraid. But, she keeps me on track and I need that. We all need that, you know...

*(**JOHNNY** nods.)*

JOHNNY. Yeah.. Wish I would've found someone to be afraid of. *(**JOHNNY** contemplates.)* Gina was mean. She was really mean. But you know, she couldn't help it. She knew what was going on with my dad and his cheating and my mom putting up with it. All the beatings. It was all on her. You know?

(**RUDY** *nods. Silence.* **JOHNNY** *takes out his guitar and starts to strum.* **JOHNNY** *looks at the envelope on the table.*)

Still haven't opened the envelope, huh?

RUDY. We don't want to know...

JOHNNY. You have to open it, Rudy. He bought life insurance in case this happened. He bought it for you and Gina and Valentina. You have to honor his wishes.

RUDY. I can't...

JOHNNY. You want me to? I will.

RUDY. No, that's okay.

(**RUDY** *drinks.* **JOHNNY** *sings, "Don't Let the Sun Catch You Crying."**)

(**JOHNNY** *sings the first verse.**)

(**JOHNNY** *and* **RUDY** *sing the second verse.**)

(**RUDY** *reaches for the envelope. He holds it. Then, he opens it.*)

(**JOHNNY** *sings the third verse.**)

(**RUDY** *reads.*)

(**JOHNNY** *sings the fourth verse.**)

(**RUDY** *drinks. He cries.*)

End of Act One

---

* Please see Music Use Note on page 3

ACT TWO

Scene One

(Footage: coverage of the Papal Conclave, April 18, 2005)

(Lights up on the ESPERANZA *talking to* EMILIANO. *She is smoking and they are drinking tequila.)*

EMILIANO. It's not boring. It's...everything.

ESPERANZA. Ah, no, you have to get more specific than that. Is it hot, is it cold, is dark, is it light?

EMILIANO. You just don't get it, *Nana.* You can't. Your mind and your soul are too small, too tiny to even imagine. You see it's so immense that this earth, no, this universe is like a speck, like a grain of sand in comparison. And everyone is there *Nana.* I mean everyone who has left this earth. They're all there. Your mother, your father, your brother... Auntie Faith, Auntie Charity, my Grandma Elena and my Grandpa Carlos...

ESPERANZA. Carlos? He's up there? Then, I guess it's true. You can be an asshole all your life, but if you repent at the end, God will forgive. *¿Así de grande es su amor? (Is God's love that big?)*

EMILIANO. *Sí, Nana.* Don't you want to see your husband, my *Tata?*

ESPERANZA. See him? I can't get rid of him! What about *La Virgen*, is she there?

EMILIANO. Yes, but she's not the way you imagine.

ESPERANZA. Is the little angel at her feet?

EMILIANO. There are angels all over, *Nana*. But, they are nothing like you imagine. All the paintings and sculptures, you know, Michelangelo and DaVinci...

(He shakes his head and laughs.)

Honestly, we don't know what true beauty is down here. We don't know what tranquility is. We don't know what true peace is. And we don't know what love is. We don't.

(Silence. He drinks his tequila.)

Help my mother, *Nana*. She's become cold and bitter.

ESPERANZA. She's always been mean, *hijo (son)*. Even when she was young.

(He laughs.)

EMILIANO. Yeah, she's always been tough. But, *Nana*, this is different.

ESPERANZA. She doesn't think I can help her. When you get old, *hijo, (son,)* people stop listening to you, like you never lived.

EMILIANO. But, didn't you say that life goes on?

ESPERANZA. Yes, it does, *hijo*. And it will...

Scene Two

(**RUDY**, **BOBBY** and **JUAN FRANCISCO** are sitting at the table. **JUAN FRANCISCO** is dressed in tight jeans, a bright shirt and he has product in his hair, just like **BOBBY**. As **JUAN FRANCISCO** tells **RUDY** about his latest adventures, **BOBBY** listens like a proud father.)

JUAN FRANCISCO. And in front of the Grauman's Chinese Theater I saw the hand prints of Marilyn Monroe. Uncle Bobby's friend sings at a night club and he dresses like Marilyn Monroe.

BOBBY. (to **RUDY**) You remember Rubén? Calls himself Ruby?

RUDY. Oh, yeah.

JUAN FRANCISCO. Uncle Bobby says he's going to take me to see him…her…

BOBBY. As soon as he turns twenty-one..

RUDY. How is it going over at the shop?

JUAN FRANCISCO. It is fine. Everyone who works there is gay…

BOBBY. …but very nice.

JUAN FRANCISCO. I like them. I never had any gay friends in *México*. You know, people in *México* are so…backward. I called my mother and told her about my job and Bobby and all my gay friends.

(**BOBBY** laughs.)

BOBBY. Tell him what she said.

(**FRANKIE** hesitates.)

Go on, tell him!

JUAN FRANCISCO. She said *"¡Ay hijo, por favor, no me vayas a salir puto!"* (*"Oh, son, please don't turn into a fag!"*) She is so homophobic, you know?

(He shakes his head in disapproval. **BOBBY** and **RUDY** crack up.)

BOBBY. Isn't that hilarious!?

JUAN FRANCISCO. All the guys in the shop, they think I am gay, too.

BOBBY. Hello?

JUAN FRANCISCO. I don't care. It is better that way, no? They are always flirting with me. But, Uncle Bobby takes care of me. He tells them...

BOBBY. You can look, but don't touch. He's my nephew. Lay off..

JUAN FRANCISCO. Now, they call Bobby my *"Papi."*

(**BOBBY** *laughs.*)

BOBBY. They do?

JUAN FRANCISCO. Yes! They are such teasers, you know.

BOBBY. Can you believe that shit?

JUAN FRANCISCO. It's okay. I like working there. It is better then waiting on a corner by the Home Depot.

BOBBY. That's for sure! *(He looks at his watch.)* Oh, shoot, I gotta go! I have a hot date tonight!

JUAN FRANCISCO. Bobby, are you going to get your groove on?

(**BOBBY** *laughs.*)

BOBBY. Gonna get it on and off, I hope! *(to* **RUDY***)* Isn't he hilarious? Okay, I'm out of here. See you tomorrow, Frankie.

JUAN FRANCISCO. Okay.

(**BOBBY** *exits stage left.*)

Everything is so different here, you know. I love my L.A. family!

(silence)

Bobby told me all about Emiliano. I'm sorry that he died. He told me that my *tía* doesn't want to open the life insurance envelope because she doesn't want to know how much her son's life was worth.

(**RUDY** *nods.*)

RUDY. That's right. But, I did. I opened it.

JUAN FRANCISCO. You did? Does she know?

RUDY. No, I haven't told her.

JUAN FRANCISCO. How much was it?

RUDY. Four hundred thousand dollars.

JUAN FRANCISCO. Four hundred thousand dollars?

RUDY. Yes, it was just like him to take out as much insurance as he could, just in case. He was a good kid.

JUAN FRANCISCO. Yes, all of the men in our family are good. That is what my *tía* says. And the women have very big mouths because they cannot lie. She says it's a curse.

(He calculates in his head.)

Four hundred thousand dollars? It is a lot of money, isn't it?

RUDY. Yes. But, it doesn't change anything.

JUAN FRANCISCO. Of course not. *(silence)* Four hundred thousand dollars… *(pause)* Can you buy a house with Four hundred thousand dollars?

RUDY. *(pause)* Yeah, you can buy a house.

JUAN FRANCISCO. I would buy a house for my mother… I would send for her first; for her and my brother and…

RUDY. You wouldn't be here to do all that, Frankie. Do you understand that the reason we have the money is because *Miliano* is dead?

(silence)

JUAN FRANCISCO. Oh… Yes, I understand. *(silence)* ¿*Tío?*

(RUDY *looks at* **JUAN FRANCISCO** *"What now?")*

Are you upset because they didn't find weapons of mass destruction?

RUDY. Yes, I'm upset. I don't believe in war. I went to Vietnam, I never wanted that for my son. Never.

JUAN FRANCISCO. Then why did you let him go?

RUDY. He didn't ask for our permission. He just went and enlisted and came home and told us. He was so proud and I couldn't bring myself to tell him how disappointed I was. We wanted him to go to college and maybe that's why he joined because he knew how expensive it is. I remember him saying one time, "Dad, if you can only afford to send one of us, send *Valentina*, she's the smart one." I don't know. One time I asked him what his plan for the future was... It was just a question, though. He knew we were against the war. He knew. I mean, we took him to anti-war rallies for Christ's sake.

JUAN FRANCISCO. But, why, *tío?* Isn't it your duty to defend your country? To protect your liberty? To die for your country? I mean Vietnam was one thing, but what about 9/11?

RUDY. They lied to us, Frankie. It's no secret. The president, the generals, the CIA, they all lied. They all lied and my son is dead.

(**JUAN FRANCISCO** *looks confused.*)

JUAN FRANCISCO. So, you don't love your country?

RUDY. What are you, a Republican? I do love it. Questioning doesn't mean I don't love it.

JUAN FRANCISCO. But, it's better than *México*. Here you don't live in fear of being killed for no reason. If it were not better than *México* then everyone would not want to be here instead of there.

(**JUAN FRANCISCO** *stands and paces. He doesn't understand and he is frustrated.*)

Tío, this is a very important question. When *México* and the U.S. play soccer who are you for?

RUDY. *México.*

JUAN FRANCISCO. I am for the U.S.! You are ungrateful, *tío.* You don't know how lucky you are!

RUDY. Lucky?

JUAN FRANCISCO. In *México* if you die for your country, you are dead and that's all! People in *México* are so proud, "¡*Qué viva México cabrones!*" ("*Long live México, assholes!*") But, they have nothing, no opportunity, no rights!

RUDY. Sometimes, we feel the same way here, too.

(silence)

JUAN FRANCISCO. You know what the difference between the people from *México* and the people from here is?

RUDY. What's that?

JUAN FRANCISCO. The people from *México*, we know we are screwed but we are still hopeful. We have dreams of a better life and we are willing to work hard for it. We come here and we will clean your house, take care of your children, change your mother's diaper, we will sell oranges or cherries or flowers or peanuts or wash your cars or sweep up your hair. We will do it, because we believe in the future.

(pause)

Here… Here you know you are screwed but you are so cynical. It is like you have accepted it as your fate. I notice it in your expressions: "Yeah, right," "Sure," "Whatever." I hate that every time somebody says something they end it with "whatever." Like you are giving up. Like you are defeated.

*(**RUDY** sits on that thought for a moment.)*

RUDY. I can't remember the last time we were optimistic. In the '60s and the '70s maybe. When JFK was president in the '60s. We were optimistic then. And in the '70s when we thought we could change the world.

JUAN FRANCISCO. I love the '70s! The music. The clothes. Jimmy Hendrix…

RUDY. You like Jimi Hendrix?

JUAN FRANCISCO. Oh, yes… I love Purple Haze…

*(**RUDY** goes to the stereo.)*

…Foxy Lady…Fire…

RUDY. "Let me stand next to your fire…"

(**RUDY** *finds a Jimmy Hendrix CD and puts it on.* "*Purple Haze*" *comes on.**)

(**RUDY** *plays air guitar and sings along.*)

(**RUDY** *sings the first four lines.**)

(**JUAN FRANCISCO** *sings the fifth line.**)

(*They both play air guitar.*)

JUAN FRANCISCO/RUDY. Na na na, na na na…

(*They fall out laughing.* **GINA** *enters. They stop. Rudy turns off the music.*)

RUDY. Hey, Gina, Frankie likes Jimmy Hendrix.

(**GINA**'s *upset.*)

You okay?

(**VALENTINA** *enters.*)

VALENTINA. Juanfra, *Nana* wants you to go up.
JUAN FRANCISCO. Okay.

(*as they walk up the stairs*)

VALENTINA. Try to make it juicy.
JUAN FRANCISCO. Juicy?
VALENTINA. *Sabroso*…
JUAN FRANCISCO. Ah…okay!
RUDY. You okay?
GINA. Yes, I said I'm okay.

(**GINA** *notices the envelope is gone.*)

RUDY. I opened it, Gina. I opened the envelope.
GINA. What? Why? Why did you do that?
RUDY. Because we had to.
GINA. Don't tell me how much it is. I don't want to know. I know you want to move on. Get on with our life. That's why you can you laugh and kid with that boy when Miliano is dead.

---

*Please see Music Use Note on page 3

RUDY. Gina, don't… Don't do this…

GINA. What are you gonna do next, spend Miliano's death money on him?

(He tries to keep his voice down.)

RUDY. You know what, Gina? I am sick and tired of you acting like you are the only one who's hurting. I'm hurting, too! But, I'll be damned if I'm going to have to prove it to you every fucking day!

*(***VALENTINA*** comes down.)*

VALENTINA. Mom, *Nana* told Juanfra that he could stay in Miliano's room!

GINA. What?

*(***GINA*** looks at ***RUDY***.)*

Damn it! I told you I didn't want him here.

*(As she goes up, ***JUAN FRANCISCO*** comes down. She walks right past him.)*

JUAN FRANCISCO. Is my *tía* okay?

*(***VALENTINA*** looks at ***RUDY***.)*

RUDY. Yeah, she's okay.

Scene Three

(ESPERANZA *is saying the Rosary:*)

ESPERANZA. *Dios te salve, María, llena eres de gracia, el Señor es contigo. Bendita tú eres entre todas las mujeres, y bendito es el fruto de tu vientre, Jesús...* (*Hail Mary full if grace, the Lord is with thee. Blessed art though amongst women and blessed is the fruit of they womb, Jesus...*)

(GINA *enters, furious.*)

GINA. Who do you think you are telling that boy that he can sleep in Miliano's room? This is my house, mine, and you have no right to say who can stay here or not! How dare you! You, you...

ESPERANZA. What? What are you going to call me? Old crazy woman? I AM THE MATRIARCH OF THIS FAMILY WHETHER YOU LIKE IT OR NOT! And as long as I am alive you will not be unkind to your relatives, to your blood!

(RUDY, VALENTINA, *and* JUAN FRANCISCO *hear the outburst.*)

GINA. He can't stay here! I don't want him here! I don't want him sleeping in Miliano's bed!

ESPERANZA. You listen to me! I know you're angry! You're mad at God for not taking care of him! You are mad at yourself for letting him go! You are mad at yourself for not saying "No! I forbid you to go to war! I forbid you to go hurt people, kill people!"

GINA. No, *Nana*, you have it all wrong. I'm mad at myself because I did! (*silence*) I tried not to... I told him I was angry with him for going and that the thought of him killing people made me sick. So, you see, he didn't have a chance. He was wounded even before he left. I hurt my son because I couldn't lie. And now he's dead.

(ESPERANZA *cries. She opens her arms to* GINA *and* GINA *goes to her.*)

Oh, *Nana*. Oh, *Nana*...

ESPERANZA. *Ay, hija, si a mí me duele, ¿cómo estarás tú que le diste vida? Ya, ya.. Llora, hija, llora.* It's good to cry. It's good to grieve. *El llanto es bueno para el espíritu. Y es un regalo de Dios. Bendita tú eres entre todas las mujeres, y bendito es el fruto de tu vientre...* (Oh, my daughter. If it hurts me, how much more must it hurt you, who gave him life. There, there... Cry, my daughter, cry. It's good to cry. It's good to grieve. To weep is good for the spirit and it is a gift from God. Blessed are you among women and blessed is the fruit of your womb...)

(Footage: black smoke from the Vatican. No Pope yet.)

(Music: "Cuatro Milpas"*)

---

* Please see Music Use Note on page 3

Scene Four

(Music: "Cuatro Milpas")

(ESPERANZA comforts GINA as SILVESTRE appears. She reaches out to him.)

(SILVESTRE sings the first verse of "Cuatro Milpas."*)

(ESPERANZA joins SILVESTRE for the second and third verses.*)

(As the song continues:)

(JUAN FRANCISCO enters the living room with his suitcase and says goodbye to RUDY and VALENTINA. JUAN FRANCISCO walks out the door.)

(ESPERANZA looks up and SILVESTRE is gone.)

ESPERANZA. Silvestre! Silvestre!

(SILVESTRE appears.)

Abrázame... abrázame... (Hold me... hold me...)

(He holds her.)

SILVESTRE. *Ya, ya... (There, there...)*

(The images of her mind return: death, wounded, carnage, weeping women. We hear her labored breath.)

Scene Five

(**GINA**, **RUDY**, **BOBBY**, **BETTY** and **VALENTINA** *are in the living room.* **GINA** *sits on the couch.*)

BOBBY. Why didn't you call me?

RUDY. He said he was going to your house. How was I supposed to know he wouldn't?

BETTY. Maybe he went back to Mexico.

BOBBY. Why would he do that?

BETTY. I mean, after Gina kicked him out.

GINA. I didn't kick him out!

VALENTINA. You might as well have.

RUDY. Valentina!

VALENTINA. Well, it's true.

BOBBY. He liked it here. He liked working at the shop…

BETTY. Without papers…

BOBBY. Shut up!

BETTY. I'm just saying…

BOBBY. Well, don't say anything unless it's relevant.

GINA. That's too much to ask.

BETTY. What I'm saying is maybe he got picked up by immigration.

RUDY. He has a visa…

BETTY. But, I thought…

GINA. Shut up…

RUDY. (*explaining to* **BETTY**) He has a tourist visa, not a working visa.

BETTY. Oh…

RUDY. They wouldn't deport him unless they found him working…

BOBBY. And he didn't go back to work.

VALENTINA. Maybe he's at a Home Depot someplace.

BOBBY. Don't say that, Valentina! They'd eat him alive out there.

(**BETTY**'s *still confused.*)

BETTY. So, what happened, exactly?

BOBBY. Betty…

BETTY. I'm just asking…

VALENTINA. My Mom got mad because *Nana* told Juanfra…

BETTY. Juanfra?

BOBBY. Frankie…

BETTY. Oh… What did *Nana* tell Franjua?

VALENTINA. That he could sleep in Miliano's room and Mom got mad.

BETTY. Well, what's wrong with that? I mean the room is empty…

BOBBY. Betty, those electroshock treatments really messed you up, didn't they?

BETTY. Don't start with me, Bobby!

BOBBY. You don't start with me, Betty!

RUDY. Okay, take it easy…

VALENTINA. Aunt Betty's right!

BETTY. I am?

VALENTINA. The room is empty and Miliano wouldn't have cared…

GINA. But, I do! I do, okay! I don't want anybody sleeping in his room because I want to go in there whenever I want to… I don't want anyone in there.

VALENTINA. Yeah, and it's all about what you want, isn't it, Mom?

RUDY. Valentina, stop!

VALENTINA. Why, Dad? It's true! It's all about Mom and what she wants and nobody can disagree with her or tell her anything because she's the only one grieving, right? Well, guess what, Mom? We're all grieving. I lost my only brother, Dad lost his only son and everybody's tiptoeing around you because they're afraid of you!

RUDY. That's enough, Valentina!

VALENTINA. It's true, Dad!

RUDY. Shut up! Shut your mouth, little girl!

(VALENTINA is shocked by RUDY's outburst. RUDY catches himself. He looks at everyone.)

Please, just leave Gina alone. Nobody is hurting more than Emiliano's mother... Nobody... Not even me.

(He embraces GINA and she cries.)

Shhh... Shhh... It's okay, baby. It's okay...

(He looks at BOBBY and BETTY.)

I'm sorry about Frankie. But, we can't deal with that right now, okay?

Scene Six

(The images continue in **ESPERANZA**'s *mind. She cries.)*

SILVESTRE. *¿Por qué lloras? (Why are you crying?)*

ESPERANZA. I'm crying for our children, for our grandchildren, for our great grandchildren. They are so removed from their ancestors, so far... They no longer know who they are. They don't know where they come from or where they are going. They don't know how to live upon the earth.

SILVESTRE. It's the path that God gave them.

ESPERANZA. No, it's the path we gave them!

SILVESTRE. And it's good. Look at them...

ESPERANZA. They're not even Mexican anymore...

SILVESTRE. *¿Y qué tiene? (What's wrong with that?)* They're different, yes. But, in their heart, Mexican, always. They are not like us. They are different. The same way we are different from our parents and our grandparents. But, the lineage continues and that is good and it is beautiful... Things change. Nothing stays the same. That's the law of life.

ESPERANZA. But, the ancient words are lost. I can't remember them. The Words of the Elders... That's why I have to stay because I am their history, I am their root and without the root the spirit dies.

Scene Seven

(There is a pounding. **RUDY** *answers the door.)*

RUDY. Frankie? What happened?

*(***JUAN FRANCISCO*** enters. He is bloodied up.)*

VALENTINA. Oh my God... Mom!

*(***GINA*** enters.)*

ESPERANZA. *(offstage)* Juan Francisco!

GINA. What happened?

*(***JUAN FRANCISCO*** tries to smile, but he looks frightened.)*

JUAN FRANCISCO. I am so sorry to cause you trouble. I went to Uncle Bobby's, but he was not home. I didn't know where else to go.

GINA. Are you okay? Who did this to you?

JUAN FRANCISCO. I was asleep in a park and these guys... I don't know why they beat me up. I gave them everything I had... They started pushing me and calling me names...wetback, queer...

*(***JUAN FRANCISCO*** looks at **RUDY**.)*

RUDY. It's okay, you can stay here.

*(***JUAN FRANCISCO*** looks at **GINA**.)*

GINA. Yes, you can stay here.

JUAN FRANCISCO. I will sleep on the sofa. It is very comfortable.

VALENTINA. I'll get the blankets.

*(***VALENTINA*** exits.)*

*(***RUDY**, **GINA** and **JUAN FRANCISCO*** stand looking at each other for a second. Then −)*

GINA. Are you hungry?

*(***VALENTINA*** enters with blankets.)*

JUAN FRANCISCO. No, no, it's okay, *tía. (aunt')*

RUDY. Are you sure?

    (**JUAN FRANCISCO** *nods shyly.*)

JUAN FRANCISCO. Maybe a little milk…

    (Footage: Habemos Papam! The Pope has been chosen.)

Scene Eight

(**ESPERANZA** *is in her room.*)

ESPERANZA. A German Pope! *¡No puede ser! Y tan feíto que está...* (*It can't be! And he's so ugly...*)

Scene Nine

(JUAN FRANCISCO *is lying down on the couch in dim light.* GINA *enters and sits close by.*)

GINA. Juan Francisco, I'm so sorry…

JUAN FRANCISCO. No, *tía. (aunt)* I am…

GINA. I shouldn't have said what I said…

JUAN FRANCISCO. But, you can't help it…

GINA. I'm still dealing with Miliano being gone…

JUAN FRANCISCO. I understand, *tía…* You need… (*He struggles for the word.*) …closure.

GINA. Yes… I wish… There's so much I wish I could say to him.

JUAN FRANCISCO. (*curious*) Like what, *tía?*

(*She looks at* JUAN FRANCISCO.)

What would you say to him?

(*A light comes up on* EMILIANO *in the* ESPERANZA's *room.*)

Say it, *tía.* He will hear you.

(GINA *speaks to* EMILIANO.)

GINA. I love you, son, and you were the best son a mother could have. I thank God for the time he gave me with you.

JUAN FRANCISCO. And he would say, "You were the best Mom in the world."

JUAN FRANCISCO/EMILIANO. "I love you, Mom."

GINA/EMILIANO. I'll see you again.

(JUAN FRANCISCO *smiles at* GINA. GINA *smiles at* JUAN FRANCISCO. *They embrace.*)

Scene Ten

(EMILIANO turns to ESPERANZA.)

EMILIANO. *Nana, ya me voy. (Nana, I'm leaving.)*

(She looks at him.)

ESPERANZA. *¿Ya? ¿Tan pronto? (Already?)*

EMILIANO. I was only here because…

ESPERANZA. I know… I'm going to miss you, my *muertito.* *(little dead one)*

EMILIANO. I'll see you soon, yes?

ESPERANZA. Yes, yes, I'll see you soon.

(He smiles.)

EMILIANO. Okay.

ESPERANZA. *Saluda a todos mis seres queridos de mi parte, ¿sí? (Say hello to all of my loved ones for me, yes?)*

EMILIANO. *Sí, Nana.*

ESPERANZA. Give my love to my mother and my father and especially to my children.

(She cries.)

Tell them I miss them and that I think of them every minute of every day.

EMILIANO. I will, *Nana.*

ESPERANZA. *Qué Dios te bendiga, hijo. (God bless you, my son.)*

EMILIANO. *Y a usted. (And you, too.)*

(EMILIANO disappears.)

Scene Eleven

(The house is decorated for a party. Signs say "Bon Voyage," "We will miss you." **RUDY**, **VALENTINA**, **BOBBY** *and* **BETTY** *are bustling about.* **RUDY** *has a beer,* **BETTY** *has a glass of wine.)*

BETTY. Then, my phone rings and I'm like, "Hello" and this woman says, "Is this '*Betty la Fea*'?"

BOBBY. What?

BETTY. His wife! It turns out he has five kids and two grandkids. I'm telling you. I'm seriously thinking about trying women.

BOBBY. So am I, at the rate I'm going.

*(**GINA** and **VALENTINA** enter from backstage. **GINA** puts a table cloth on the table with **BETTY**'s help.)*

BETTY. Is *Nana* coming down?

GINA. No, she's upset about Frankie leaving. She said for you to take her a plate up later. She wants to know what's going on with *"Pedro."*

BOBBY. He "Petered" out!

*(He laughs at his own joke. **BETTY** rolls her eyes.)*

BETTY. Oh, God.

RUDY. What's taking him so long?

GINA. She's giving him *"La Bendición."* *("The Blessing")* She's almost done.

*(**BOBBY** is sentimental.)*

BOBBY. God, I'm gonna miss him. Everybody at the shop will. He's like a son...

(pause)

... I mean, little brother.

*(**BETTY** looks at **RUDY**.)*

BETTY. Do you think he'll come back?

RUDY. Who knows. I hope so.

(JUAN FRANCISCO *comes down the stairs dressed in a military uniform. He looks handsome and very much like* EMILIANO.)

There he is.

JUAN FRANCISCO. My *tía* gave me this. (*He holds up a bottle of tequila.*) She said that we should have a toast. *Una copita (a little shot)* "for the road," she says.

VALENTINA. I'll get the glasses.

(*She goes to the bar upstage right.*)

JUAN FRANCISCO. I have been thinking about what I want to say to you and there are so many things.

(VALENTINA *hands out the shot glasses.*)

First, I want to thank you for everything you have done for me. Uncle Bobby, you gave me a job and honestly, you are more like a father to me.

(BOBBY *tears up.*)

BOBBY. Father? Well, okay...

(JUAN FRANCISCO *smiles.*)

JUAN FRANCISCO. And my *tío (uncle)* Rudy... Thank you for all the talks and for explaining so many things to me.

(*He looks at* GINA.)

Tía, (Aunt,) I know it has been hard for you to have me here and I understand why. And I know that you are both probably disappointed because I joined the Army because of your anti-war philosophy... But, I have great hope in the future and I have always wanted to see the middle east and I believe that I will come back and become a citizen and make a future here with my mother and my brother and I will have a family of my own and live the American Dream that I have heard so much about. And if I don't make it...

(*He pulls an envelope out of his jacket inside pocket.*)

At least I know that my mother and my brother will be okay.

(He hands the envelope to **BOBBY**.)

BOBBY. *Tío* Bobby, will you hold on to this for me?

*(***BOBBY*** *takes it.*)

JUAN FRANCISCO. Thank you.

*(***RUDY*** *pours the tequila.* **GINA** *holds up her glass.*)

GINA. Frankie. Juan Francisco. You know I can't lie. But, I know why you are doing this and I understand.

JUAN FRANCISCO. Thank you, *tía.* And now, let's be good Mexicans and drink our *tequila! (He holds up his glass.)* To hope and to the future.

ALL. ¡*Salud! (Cheers!)*

(They drink.)

VALENTINA. Okay, everybody. I have a surprise for you all. Well, for Frankie...

*(***VALENTINA*** *gets the guitar.*)

Okay, *Nana* has been wanting me to learn this song and I finally did...

(She begins to strum the guitar and sings the first verse of "Canción Mixteca.")*

(as the song continues softly...)

---

*Please see Music Use Note on page 3

Scene Twelve

(Upstairs, **ESPERANZA** *calls out.)*

ESPERANZA. *¡Silvestre! ¡Silvestre ven! (Silvestre! Silvestre come!)*

(SILVESTRE *appears.)*

Ya me acordé. (I remember.) I remember the words. The words of the old people. What I kept forgetting. *La antigua palabra... (The ancient words of wisdom...)*

(She remembers the words that her grandmother blessed her with so many years before.)

You have arrived, my little girl; precious necklace, precious feather; You came to life. You were born. Our Creator and our Mother sent you to earth. This is a place of thirst, a place of hunger. This is how things are. Listen and learn how to live upon the earth. How should you live? Remember, that one does not live easily upon this earth. But, do not forget that above all, you have come from someone; that your are descended from someone; that you were born by the grace of someone; that you are both the spine and the offspring of our ancestors; of those who came before us and of those who have gone on to live in the great beyond.

Scene Thirteen

(**SILVESTRE** *looks at* **ESPERANZA**.)

SILVESTRE. *¿Ya? (Now?)*

(*She looks at him.*)

Are you coming or not?

ESPERANZA. Yes, yes.. I'm going…

(*She begins to get up and then – *)

No, I'd better not.

SILVESTRE. *Ay, mujer… (Oh, woman…)*

ESPERANZA. What will they do without me? And who will take care of Valentina and her children?

SILVESTRE. Her mother, Gina, will take care of them.

ESPERANZA. No, I mean after Gina dies. Valentina will need me. That big mouth of hers is going to cause her a lot of problems.

SILVESTRE. *Pero, Esperanza… (But, Esperanza…)*

ESPERANZA. Stay here with me just a little longer.

(*She reaches out to him, he takes her hand and sits next to her as they listen to their grandchildren and great grandchild sing "Canción Mixteca" by José López Alavez.**)

(*Music and lights fade out.*)

End of Play

---

*Please see Music Use Note on page 3

CPSIA information can be obtained
at www.ICGtesting.com
Printed in the USA
BVHW081649090819
555531BV00010B/226/P